My special thanks to
to Sharon Ellison, Editor

Also my thanks to
Adry Wheeler for use
of his horse even
if she did buck
Clay Collins off while
we were shooting the cover

Other titles in the
Settling the West Series

The Forbes Family
and
Lance Burkholt

Settling The West Series
Commodore Kelley

Copyright © 2015 by David Dodge

ISBN 978-1-890548-23-0
Masair publications

Published in the United States of America
Januarary 2016

Printed by
Southwest Direct Inc.
southwestdirect.com

Cover Design By
Isaac Munoz
isaacmunozsr@yahoo.com

Commodore Kelley

Chapter One

It was the spring of 1889. A lone rider eased his long-tailed mustang down a hill outside the little town of Sykesville, Texas, just south of the Goodnight-Loving Trail. He rode slowly down the main street. As his horse moved along, he threw his hooves slightly outward giving the appearance of 'prancing', and as he did, little puffs of dust rose from the street that had not yet been watered down for the day.

From every doorway the townsfolk watched him slowly go by. In the saddle he appeared to be tall. He had a dark complexion with silvery blue eyes; he hadn't shaved in days, which added to the mystery. His hat was black, as was his long coat that covered his war bag.

The whispers from behind the partially opened doors of the livery stable were positive he was a new gambler hired by the Gentlemen's Retreat saloon to continue skinning the honest citizens.

Some of the ladies standing near Neal Johnson's store watched his entrance into town. They were sure he was the new preacher here to take the place of Brother Fredericks who was to leave for a congregation in Oregon City, Texas, next month.

The rider continued down the center of the street, never looking to the right or to the left.

When he reached the Sheriff's office, he turned to the hitching rack, stepped down, flipped the reins over it and walked inside.

This action would have spoiled the imagined destination of the handsome stranger, but for the known fact that gamblers must report to the Sheriff before they practice their trade in Sykesville.

A man who had been watching him from across the street said, "See there Barney, I told ye so!"

"What? Stoppin' in the Sheriff's office? That don't tell me nothin'!"

Inside Sheriff Bob Lacey's office, the tall stranger removed his hat and announced, "Sheriff Lacey, my name is Commodore Kelley."

The Sheriff's hair was grayed at the temples he was tall and thin, and his smile showed just below his thick mustache. He turned, stood and extended his hand. "I'm glad to meet you Mister Kelley. I'm Bob Lacey, what can I do for you?"

"Well, it's what I can do for you Sheriff. I've been re-assigned as Marshall to this district by President Hayes, because of the problems with rustling and the fact that the rustlers seem to slip past the federal judge here."

"That's true, Marshall. I've caught several rustlers but can't seem to get a conviction!"

"My job here is to assist you in changing that."

"How do you purpose we do that and what about Marshall Claxton?" asked Sheriff Lacey.

"Marshall Claxton's four years are up. That's why I've been assigned here. I guess technically he's still Marshall until I relieve him. With your help I plan to start seeing how many of his deputies, clerks, and anyone else, all the way up to the judge himself, can or should be changed!"

"You say the President sent you here?"'

"Yes. It seems a couple of ranchers around here, Roscoe and Hawk, are friends of his. He wants it taken care of."

"That sure sounds good to me!" said Sheriff Lacey, "I've found that the defense lawyers have little trouble convincin' Judge Hargrove of their client's innocence."

"That's one thing I want to look into, but I guess the first thing I ought to do is to find a place to stay."

"Well, I can recommend Annie Shaw's boardin' house. She serves a mighty good meal and . . . is easy on the eyes."

"That'll be fine. Maybe later I can get a little place of my own. For awhile, let's just say I'm a stranger in town. "

"I can do that, Marshall. If you rode through town, your occupation could be most anything and everybody is sure of it," he said with a chuckle.

"And . . . for right now, just call me Gus."

Commodore Kelley left the Sheriff's office and headed toward the boarding house.

Gus, as he is called, served four years as Marshall for president Ulysses S. Grant and was reinstated for another four years under Rutherford B. Hayes. He had been assigned to the district that includes Sykesville because of the unprocessed rustling complaints that had been brought against the federal judge in this area.

Gus' duties were to take care of everything involved with the court. At this time he wasn't sure it was the judge's fault. That was part of what he was supposed to find out.

As he left the Sheriff's office, the new spring leaves on the cottonwood trees rattled in the gentle breeze. He stepped up on the long porch of the boarding house and headed toward the door. The rhythmic sounds of his boots and spurs across the porch awoke a couple of old timers who had dozed off while watching the morning traffic. It was still early, and across the street kids were laughing and playing as they trekked toward the school house at the edge of town.

When he entered the open door, before him stood the loveliest young lady he had ever seen standing behind the counter. The sun shone through an open window behind her, lighting her golden hair. When she smiled, her blue eyes sparkled. Gus melted and could hardly speak.

Gus placed his gear on the floor and looked down, trying to recover from having his breath taken away. He straightened and said, "Good mornin', Miss Shaw. I assume you are Miss Annie Shaw."

"I am, and what can I do for you Mister . . . err, ah . . . "

Gus quickly answered, "Kelley, Commodore Kelley. Folks call me Gus . . . I guess it's easier to remember Gus than Commodore."

"Oh, I don't know . . . I kinda like Commodore! It's not a name you hear often. Now, what can I do for you, Mister Kelley?"

Gus blushed when she said she liked his name, "Please, just call me Gus. I need a place to stay, as I plan to work in your fair settlement for a while."

"Would you want to include meals? If you plan to stay awhile, they will be included."

"Well count me here for a while; I don't know how long it will take to finish the work I have to do here, but I will need to eat."

"Oh? And what work would that be, Mister Kelley?"

"I can't say right now. I'm still thinkin' about it, Miss Shaw"

Not wanting to pry she said, "Well, since you are a boarder now, you must call me Annie."

"I thank you, ma'am. I wouldn't mind havin' a room upstairs overlookin' the street; I kinda like to see what's going on in town."

"I can do that, Gus," she smiled at him. He melted again. "And when you get settled in, you'll find we are still serving breakfast."

"Thank you, ma'am; that's just what I need!"

Gus settled into his room, washed up, combed his hair and headed to the dining room for breakfast. While he studied the list of selections for breakfast he was unaware of the two who were watching him. Harve Tobeck, the cook, a little man with beady eyes asked Annie, "Who's the new guy at table three?"

As she watched Gus, she answered, "His name is Commodore Kelley . . . but I didn't find out anything about him . . . he said he couldn't say."

Harve looked puzzled. "He couldn't say?"

"No, not right now, anyway."

"That's sorta strange, isn't it?" Harve asked.

"Not as far as I'm concerned, maybe he's still looking for a job. He is handsome, isn't he?"

"I wouldn't know about that," said Harve as he rolled his eyes and turned back into the kitchen.

With that settled she set about serving Gus coffee.

Chapter Two

Gus wanted to become familiar with the country around Sykesville, so he increased his supplies and rode for three days.

Sheriff Lacey had given him a rough map of the locations of the ranches and their owners. His horse, Pepper, still had plenty of energy and was ready to move out. Pepper was a black mustang taken from the plains of Northern New Mexico when he was only a colt. Pepper and Gus had been together all his life. He may have been ready to continue on, but Gus was ready for a bath, a good meal, and a bed.

Seeing Gus riding near his place a time or two, a rancher named Rice Stanford became curious. He immediately sent a message to Harve Tobeck, the cook at the boarding house, to come to his place that evening after his work was finished.

When Harve arrived at the Stanford ranch, he immediately went to the den where Rice was waiting. Rice was an impressive man. His voice seemed to boom, and his presence filled the room. As Harve entered, Rice turned and addressed him. "I understand that a new man is in town and is stayin' at the boardin' house."

"Yes, sir, he came in three or four days ago."

"What's his business here?" Rice demanded.

"Well . . . nobody knows why he's in town, and I figured he'd leave in a day or two. Maybe he's a gunfighter. He was dressed in black."

"Gunfighter?"

"Well, sir, I didn't say he was a gunfighter. I said he might be! He could be a lawman, or a gambler, 'cause he did stop in at the Sheriff's office when he first came into town."

"Well, find out what you can, and keep me informed. I don't like people comin' into town when I don't know why," said Rice.

"I will, Mister Stanford," he answered, afraid to disagree.

Next day at work, while Annie was waiting on Harve to finish an order, he mentioned being summoned to the Stanford ranch.

"What did Rice want with you?" she asked.

"He wanted to know about the stranger in town."

"What business is it of his? He's always sticking his nose into everybody's business! What did you tell him?"

"Nothin' I could tell him . . . I didn't know nothin'."

"Better keep it that way . . . Rice has ways to get you obligated to him," warned Annie.

"He always wants me to keep him informed about everybody that's new and stays here. He thinks I'm where I can find out about everybody," said Harve.

"You would do well to watch what you tell him." She left to serve the breakfast.

"Good morning, Mister Kelley . . . er, uh . . . Gus!"

"And a good mornin' to you too, Miss Shaw . . . or is it Mrs.?"

"No, it's still Miss. Not many prospects of it changing here in Sykesville."

10

Gus' heart raced a little, "I would'a thought most of the men in town would be on your door step."

"You are too kind, Gus. What are you having for breakfast, this morning?"

"Well, I'd be hard pressed to find anything better than what you've served me the last few mornin's."

"That it is, then, Mister Kelley", she turned and went back into the kitchen.

From his vantage point, Gus watched her move in and around the kitchen, admiring her beautiful figure, wondering if he could get to know her better outside of the boarding house.

Meanwhile at the Stanford ranch, Rice had called for his foreman, Blake Conway, a muscular man with pale blue eyes, square chin and an unruly shock of blond hair. When he arrived, Rice said, "Blake, I've asked that cook of Annie's to let me know about the stranger that's come to town; he didn't know anything, and I don't trust him to find out much. So, I want you to send that new man . . . what's his name?"

"Tiny Marsh," said Blake.

"Yea, he's dependable idn't he?"

"You can count on Tiny; why?"

"We keep a room in the back of the Gentleman's Retreat. Tell him to go in and tell Louise I want him to stay there in town for a while to listen for information on this new man in town. This'll cover the boardin' house and the saloon. We ought'a be able to find out what his angle is that way. He may be a gunfighter hired by one of them big ranches, or he could be a lawman. I don't think he's a gambler, 'cause he hasn't gone in the Gentlemen's Retreat yet.

Whatever, I don't want him pokin' around. There's enough folk in town who think we rustle the cattle that's gone missing and with a stranger ridin' around my place, they'll think he works for me!"

"Okay, boss, I'll send Marsh right away."

During dinner at the boarding house that evening, Annie was serving the second round of after-dinner coffee to Gus as he sat quietly at the corner table.

"Why don't you sit a while, Annie; you've been buzzin' around like a little bee all evenin'."

"I'll just do that, Gus!" She placed the hot coffee pot on a plate and sat down in the extra chair. "Gus, you seem to be causing quite a stir in our little community."

"Oh? How's that?" Gus inquired.

"Well, it seems a local ranch owner by the name of Rice Stanford is interested in finding out just why you're in town."

"Others, too, or so I've been told," he replied.

"Yes, and that includes me!" she reacted. "How come I haven't found out?"

"I guess you just haven't spent enough time with me to find out. Anyway, what makes you think this Rice Stanford is interested in me?"

"He's got my cook running back and forth to his ranch with anything he can find out about you."

"Now, why do you suppose he wants to know about me?"

"I've suspected for a long time that he knows who does all the cattle rustling around here, and he's probably right in the middle of it. Some of his hands have been tried but not convicted. He is probably afraid you may be here to interfere!" she explained.

He smiled a little devilish smile. "I understand there's a dance tonight at the church . . . I might be willing to confide in you if you'll go with me."

She squinted her eyes at Gus, "Isn't that considered black mail?"

"Not by me. I'd consider it a journey for curiosity satisfaction!" he said. She saw his eyes sparkle as he smiled again.

"I'll consider it, Mister Kelley." She left to get more coffee.

Gus finished his coffee then went to his room.

Gus had just come back to his room after a bath and shave, when he heard a knock at the door. He had picked up a clean shirt, and was getting ready to put it on, as he said, "Come in." He turned and saw Annie standing in the doorway.

Annie saw his broad shoulders and muscular chest. A thrill rushed through her body.

Seeing it was Annie, he quickly slipped the shirt on, and then finished buttoning it up. The white shirt accented the red flush of his face. "I'm sorry. I was getting dressed for the dance, and I thought it was that fellow that cleans. Come in and sit down."

"Oh, don't apologize; maybe I enjoyed it," she blushed then said, "Now where did that come from?"

Gus chuckled.

She watched him for a minute. "I was checking to see if that invitation to the dance still holds."

He turned to her with a smile, "Yes it does, and I see you have turned yourself into the top candidate for queen of the ball."

She smiled, "It might just turn out that I'm with the king of the ball!"

Gus blushed again, so he turned away, picked up his coat, and ushered her out the door.

When they arrived at the church the music hadn't started, so most couples were standing around the edges of the dance floor enjoying punch and conversation. As Gus and Annie entered, all eyes were on them. Annie whispered, "There will be tongues wagging tomorrow!"

"You know they'll think you know me, or that you're just a 'hussy'," he joked.

"I like being the talk of the town once in a while, but I hope they don't think that."

"You may change your mind once I tell you why I'm in your town," he suggested.

"Oh? It's that bad, is it?"

"Rice Stanford may think so."

Annie just looked at him with a puzzled look on her face. The music started, so Gus swept her up and spun around the dance floor. It happened so quickly that they were the only ones on the floor for a few minutes. Folks watched, smiled, and clapped their hands to the music.

She pushed Gus back a little. So she could look him in the eye, "Boy, when you start dancing . . . you start dancing!"

"I want to get in as much time as I can with the prettiest lady at the dance," said Gus. "And I want them to see that she's with me."

Annie put her cheek to his so he couldn't see how much she was blushing.

"Everyone else on the dance floor are married couples. The girls standing around are single . . . you should ask some of them to dance, so you can get to know others who live here in Sykesville." She said trying to make conversation.

"Are you trying to get rid of me?"

"No, I just wanted you to get acquainted with some of the folks," she answered.

"You don't think I'll get my head knocked off do you?"

"Gus, this is a friendly town. The guys are all outside drinking for a while, to get enough gumption to ask the girls to dance!"

"That's what I'm afraid of . . . drinkin' for a while."

As they danced close to the edge of the floor, Annie twirled out by one of the girls who had been watching. "Gus, I'd like you to meet LaRice Stanford, LaRice, this is Commodore Kelley."

"I'm very glad to meet you, ma'am," said Gus.

Annie looked Gus straight in the eyes and said, "LaRice is Rice Stanford's daughter."

Gus gave a very small nod toward Annie, took LaRice's hand and asked if she would like to dance. Her response was affirmative.

As they moved around the circle, Gus said, "LaRice, that's a very nice name . . . I don't believe I've heard it before."

"Probably not; it's pronounced La-*Rice* because it's like daddy's name, Rice. Daddy wanted a boy, and he had his name picked out as a junior, so he gave it to me anyway, with a bit of modification!"

"I think it's a nice name, but I can sympathize with you, since my name is Commodore."

"Yes, but at least you have a normal name for folks to call you . . . Gus, wasn't it?"

"Yeah, that's what my Dad called me."

By this time they had completed the round, so Gus politely thanked LaRice. Annie introduced him to Bernice Zink, and he was off again. By the time they had made the large dance circle, a few of the young men who had been outside, building enough courage to ask the girls to dance, were drifting in, so Gus took Annie's hand and pulled her back on the floor. "Who's the guy dancin' with LaRice now?"

Annie turned so she could see, "I think that's Tiny Marsh. He works for Rice, and the one in the blue shirt is Blake Conway, Rice's foreman."

"You mean he lets his daughter associate with the hired hands?"

"He probably requires it," she bit off.

While Tiny Marsh danced with LaRice he asked her, "I saw you dancin' with that new feller . . . what'd you find out about him?"

"I didn't find out anything, why do you ask?"

"Well, your Paw wanted me to find out why he's here."

She stopped dancing with Tiny, saying as she walked away, "You can tell Daddy he can do his own snooping."

When the dance was over Commodore and Annie walked back to the boarding house along the Concho River.

As they walked along Annie reminded Gus, "You know you haven't told me yet why you are here, and how long you are going to stay."

"I know . . . I guess I was afraid that when I told you, you might not be friendly anymore."

"What makes you think that? Do you clean out privies or deal in buffalo carcasses?"

He chuckled. "No, nothin' like that! I've been assigned as U.S. Marshall for this district," he said, watching her reaction intently.

"Marshall? What about Marshall Claxton?" she asked. "I saw him this morning."

"He's still Marshall here 'till I relieve him, but I won't do that until I find out more about what's going on around here. I'm afraid he might be in with the rustlin' that's been goin' on."

"You know about the rustling?" she quizzed.

"Yes. Two of the ranchers around here have sent a letter to the President about it; they seem to know him."

She thought a minute, then said, "I'll just bet it was Earl Roscoe and Jerald Hawk. They have the two largest ranches around . . . except for Rice. He has the largest, at least by cattle count."

"Anybody ever look at his cattle?"

"Nope! As far as I know he doesn't want anybody to come on his ranch. Gus, I really had better go in. I told Helen I wouldn't be gone long."

Gus took her hand, "Now that you know, will it make a difference?"

She smiled, "No, I don't care what your business is. I'm glad you are here. It ought to be fun to watch you work. I'd say it's not going to be a small task!"

Gus looked down as they walked along, "Now, it's your turn . . . how did you wind up in the great settlement of Sykesville?"

"Our family followed the Military. Father was a Colonel in the Army and was in charge of the horses. We were in Pennsylvania, and Father was moved to San Antonio. My older sister fell in love with a man from Sykesville. He owned the boarding house. He and his family were attacked and killed while on a trip to Oklahoma. There wasn't anyone else to take over the boarding house, so . . . I'm here."

"And I'm glad," said Gus. "Maybe we can talk more later. You know I don't want anyone to know yet."

"Commodore Kelley, your secret is safe with me. See you in the morning at breakfast." She gave him a quick kiss on the cheek. "I had fun tonight."

Gus was frozen for a moment and then finally said, "I had fun, too." He watched her walk to the front door of the boarding house and disappear inside.

He returned to the river and stood there listening to the water rushing by, reflecting on the evening's events, wondering if he had done the right thing by telling Annie why he was here in Sykesville. He wanted to be honest with her because he was sure she was the one for him. As he turned to look at the river the moon broke the horizon as a large orange ball.

He watched a minute, and then whispered, "Now you come up! Where were you when the lady was here?" He took out his watch, flipped it open, and checked the time the moon came up. He stood a while longer, then he went to his room.

In his room, he studied the maps the sheriff had given him so he could become familiar with the location of each of the ranches and their brands. When he finally looked at his watch, he had worked through the night. As it was almost time for breakfast, he washed his face, combed his hair and went to the dining room.

Annie floated out of the kitchen with trays containing several steaming breakfasts. As she passed Gus coming in the door, she said, "Why, good morning Mmmm . . . my you look rested this morning!"

Gus frowned at first when he thought she was about to call him Marshall. When she corrected herself, he smiled and took a seat.

Annie came to his table, turned over his cup and poured it full, all the time watching his face. "Gus, I'm sorry. I thought about what you told me, and it was fresh on my mind."

"It's okay, Annie, you recovered fine!"

"Same this morning?"

"Yep, hard to ride without a good breakfast."

"Will you be back for dinner?"

"I sure hope so; its roast beef tonight isn't it?"

"Yes it is. I'll pack you a lunch, if you like."

"That would be nice. I'm not sure how you'll do it, but if you can put a little honey in for those biscuits, that would be nice."

"I'll do what I can."

19

"That's all I ask," he said, and continued to watch her work. He thought as he watched, *Commodore, if you work it just right you may have found the girl you've been lookin' for.*

Before his ride that morning, he met with Judge Winston Hargrove. He did not let on that he was the replacement for Marshall Wade Claxton, or that the Judge might be moved elsewhere.

"Judge Hargrove, I was kinda interested in investing in some land around here to raise a few head of cattle. The land looks good; does anyone do any farmin' around here?"

"Nope, and most of the land that's worth anything is taken. You would be hard pressed to find anything in this area. Farmers don't last long before they move on."

"Oh? Is that by choice?" Gus asked, tongue in cheek.

His comment went over the Judge's head. "Naw, farms just don't do well in these parts."

"If I was to find some land to raise cattle on, do you have any rustlin' in these parts?"

The judge put his cigar down, "Naw, some folks claim we do, but we don't stand for it here."

"You keep a pretty tight rein on that sort of thing, I guess."

"That we do . . . that we do."

"Well, Judge. I thank you for your time." He started to rise, but the Judge had another question.

"What really brought you to this part of the country, anyway?"

"Well, I was headed west of here, but when I got to the boardin' house and saw Miss Shaw, I thought it might be a nice place to stay," said Gus.

"I see . . . what is your profession, if you don't mind my asking? We kinda frown on drifters," the Judge said, sternly.

"Oh, I'm still lookin' right now, but somethin' will come along," answered Gus.

"Well, then, Mister Kelley, I hope it does soon."

"I thank you for your time and concern, your Honor."

Later, as Gus headed back to his room, he decided to stop in at the Gentlemen's Retreat. He paused at the butterfly doors and looked in briefly, then pushed on in and walked to the bar. He stood where he could see most of the room reflected in the mirror over the bar. It was only a few minutes until Louise Webber, the manager, approached.

"Well, hello, stranger. I'm Louise and what are you called?"

"The name's Commodore Kelley, but Gus gets my attention."

"Well, welcome to the Gentlemen's Retreat, Gus. How 'bout we sit at a table, and I'll buy you a drink."

Gus eased his elbow off the bar and followed Louise to a table.

"Gus . . . tell me about yourself."

"Well, ma'am, there's not much to tell. I've been ridin' through a lot of country lately, and thought this little town looked mighty friendly, so I stopped for a while."

"Where'd you ride from . . . was it far?"

"Yes ma'am, I rode here from the far eastern edge of Virginia."

"You *have* been riding a long time. I guess you deserved to stop for a while.

She looked toward the bar and motioned toward the bartender. "Mike, bring Mister Kelley a drink, the good stuff. Now, Gus, you wouldn't happen to deal cards would you?"

Mike sat the drink on the table; Gus took it and thanked him. "No, ma'am, I'm afraid not. I've never been too good at gamblin'."

"Well, Gus, that's a shame," she said sadly. I can always use another dealer."

They visited awhile, long enough that everyone in the saloon new Gus' name. He had told her he had worked cattle and had done a little blacksmithing. After a while she had made up her mind that he was sort of a drifter.

"Well, Mister Kelley, we here in Sykesville welcome you, so don't be a stranger here at the Gentlemen's Retreat, and stay here as long as you like!"

"No ma'am, I won't, and I thank you for the drink," he responded with a wide smile.

Louise moved on to watch a card game, and Gus sat there a while studying the faces of the men in the room. He watched Rice's man, the one Annie said was Tiny Marsh, walk over to the table where Louise watched the players. *I guess Tiny will have a bit more information to give Rice,* he thought.

Soon, he decided to go back to the boarding house. It wasn't far, but Gus took his time. The bright red-orange moon was coming up and while it was close to the horizon it looked extra large. Gus watched it a while and thought, *There you are again . . . boy what a waste. I should be walkin' by the river with Annie. Guess I'll see if I can arrange that for tomorrow night.*

He always took heed of his feelings, and right now he sensed someone was near, following him from the saloon.

He eased behind a tree where the moonlight wouldn't shine on him and quickly took a survey of the area. Nothing moved, and he couldn't see anyone, so he headed on to his room, but he couldn't shake the feeling of being watched.

When he entered his room, he struck a match and brushed it across the wick of the lamp. The yellow flame flickered and slowly reached upward from the wick. As he replaced the globe it brightened into a warm glow that filled the room. He lifted the lamp and began to survey the room. Checking on the things he had placed a certain way in the room, he was sure nothing had been moved. Then he mumbled, "Gus, I think you're a little paranoid!"

Satisfied no one had gone through his things, he went to bed afraid he would be unable to go to sleep. He didn't realize how tired he was and quickly dropped into sleep.

He was never a sound sleeper, and a slight rattling of a key turning in a door-lock woke him. His hand instantly slid beneath the pillow and his fingers wrapped around the smooth ivory handle of his 44-40 Colt. He listened . . . a door opened to the room next to him, and he relaxed. Half out loud he said, "I gotta stop being so jumpy. No one knows what I have to do here," he turned over and slept soundly.

Chapter Three

As the early spring sun was struggling to rise above the horizon, it pushed a beam through the slightly raised shade on the window. That beam reached across the room and into the sleeping face of Commodore Kelley. He was quickly awake.

After a cold face wash, he dressed and headed to the dining room.

"Good morning, Mister Kelley."

"Good morning to you, Miss Shaw."

She turned his cup over and filled it. "How are you this morning?"

"First good sleep since I've been here!"

She smiled and said, "I hear you visited our facility of libation."

"If you mean the saloon, yeah, I did. I met Louise too! She even bought me a drink. How'd you know that, anyway?"

"Oh, word gets around."

"I guess it does. Kinda hard for a man to have a secret, isn't it? By the way, I've missed two nights havin' you with me when a beautiful full moon rose over the river, I don't want to make it three . . . will you help me watch it tonight?"

"Why sure, Gus, be glad to."

"I'll knock on your door about six thirty, if that's all right."

"I'll be expecting you."

"One more thing. Where can a fellow get a bit of laundry done?"

She smiled. "Charlie Wong's. His house is right behind the Sheriff's office."

After breakfast Gus gathered his clothes, left through the rear door and strolled down the alley to avoid being seen near the Sheriff's office. When he walked behind the feed store, a cat jumped from where some feed had spilled, almost causing him to draw his gun. *Getting a bit jumpy, aren't you, he* thought. He continued on until he saw the 'Laundry' sign by the door then he stepped up on the porch and knocked.

An elderly oriental man appeared; his glasses had slipped down his nose and beads of sweat covered his forehead.

"You come in, please," said Charlie Wong.

"Thank you. I need a few things done." Gus placed his clothes on the table, and Charlie started to straighten them out to count the pieces. He held up one of Gus' shirts, looked at it, and then looked at Gus.

"You lawman!" said Charlie.

A bit startled, Gus asked, "What makes you say that?"

"Holes in shut wheuh badge pin on. I do Missuh Lacey shuts."

"I see . . . you're a pretty good detective, Mister Wong. How about we let that be our little secret."

"Chawlie not talk other's business!"

"Very good, I thank you."

"You pick up in morning." Charlie said matter-of-factly.

As he left Wong's place he mumbled, "I can't believe, now, how many people know my business. Oh well, if the word gets out too quick I'll just have to live with it."

That evening after Annie finished and Helen Thomas took over the duties at the front desk, she went to her room. After a while she heard a knock. As she opened the door, Gus stood there smiling.

"Are you ready to watch that moon come up?" he asked.

"Oh Gus, I just got here, and I've had a pretty rough day. Can we watch it tomorrow?"

He hid his disappointment. "Why, sure Annie, I'm sorry you've had a rough day. Before I go, can I come in a minute?"

"Certainly."

Gus moved into the room and shut the door.

"I thought I'd pass a little information that you could 'accidentally' drop for Harve to pass along to get Rice's curiosity up even more. Tomorrow I plan to visit both Earl Roscoe and Jerald Hawk. You can let him wonder what I'm goin' for."

She showed a little smile, "That should whip him up real good!"

"Well, you get some rest; I'll see you when I get back."

"Don't stay out so long that you will be late for our moon walk," she reminded.

"You can bet I won't."

Gus was up early, and left by the back door. The alley was clear, so he walked to Sheriff Lacey's office and went in the back door.

"Good mornin', Sheriff Lacey."

"Well, good mornin', Gus. How come you came in the back door this mornin'?"

"I didn't want too many to see me visitin' you. I was wonderin' if you would have time to ride with me to Earl Roscoe's place and maybe even Jerald Hawk's. I need to talk to them and let them know about the change, and let them know, too, that we are willing to look into the legal aspects that they feel have failed them. They may listen to me if you are along . . . otherwise, they may think I'm just lookin' for a job."

"Sure, when do you want to go?"

"Do you think we can visit both places in one day?"

"Don't know why not; their headquarters are real close together."

"If we tell them now, before I really get a chance to investigate like I plan to do, do you think they can keep it quite?" asked Gus.

"They are both solid citizens, and when they find you plan to help, I think you can count on them," said Sheriff Lacey.

"Fine . . . will this mornin' be too soon?"

"No, that will be fine. Why don't we go to my place, and I'll get ready while you have some more coffee."

Gus thought a minute. "That's good, Bob. Your place is out of the way, and there will be fewer eyes to see us together as we leave town."

Sheriff Lacey started for the door, paused and turned to Gus. "I've got a new colt I want to ride. Not many people here in town have seen it, so I'll ride him. That way it won't be so easy to recognize it's me ridin' with you."

"Good idea, Sheriff! I'll see you there."

As they road toward the two ranches, Commodore asked, "If you suspect Rice of being behind the rustlin', do you think he changes the brands?"

"Most of the loss has been calves taken before they have a chance to brand them. It's like they have a man right there waitin' for a calf to drop."

"They don't take branded stock?" Gus asked.

"Oh yeah, those too!"

"Well, how do they change a brand to his brand? I don't see how he could do it."

"Rice has several brands registered. They are brands that could be made by runnin' someone else's brand. Do you understand?"

"Yes, I do. He just runs a brand over the old one and however it turns out, he registers it."

"That's the way it looks like he works it," said the Sheriff. "Course, I don't know that for sure."

"That should be pretty easy to prove, Bob."

"That's what we think, but we haven't been able to prove it in this court."

Gus rode along thinking, then a little way down the trail he said, "Bob, I'd like to have a look at Rice's cattle . . . maybe it's not him."

"I would, too, but he won't allow anyone on his place. He says he don't rustle cattle and that's that!"

"Hummm . . . I'll have to see about that!"

They topped a little rise, and looked off into the valley below. The Hawk ranch spread across the near end of the valley. The beautiful rock headquarters was surrounded by bunk houses, several pens, granaries, and barns. Not too far away was the

Roscoe Ranch down near the far end of that valley with similar facilities.

As they approached the main house, Jerald Hawk stood on the front porch drinking a cup of coffee. When he saw it was the Sheriff, he stepped off the porch toward the hitching rack.

"Mornin', Bob. What brings you out here this mornin'?"

"Good mornin', Jerald. Well, I could say I just wanted to go for a ride on a pretty mornin', but that wouldn't be true." Bob and Gus stepped down and looped their reins over the hitching rack, "I'm here to introduce you to Commodore Kelley."

Gus reached out to shake Jerald Hawk's hand. Just call me Gus, and I'm glad to meet you, Mister Hawk."

"You too, Mister Kelley. That coffee pot is still hot; pour yourselves a cup and have a seat here on the porch."

"Thanks. That'll taste real good," replied Gus.

Gus poured himself and the Sheriff a cup and they sat down.

"Mister Hawk, I wanted Sheriff Lacey to come with me because I wanted to speak with you in confidence. We're trying to keep my identity quiet for a while. President Hays got yours and Mister Roscoe's letter about your concern over the rustlin' that's takin' place here. He assigned me to be the Marshall of this district. Marshall Claxton's time is up, but I need to find out more about what's going on before any changes are made."

"Rutherford got our letter, did he? Well it's been so long I didn't know if he got it or not. I asked him to send the best help he had, 'cause it's got purdy bad out here."

"He got your letter all right. I don't know about the best he had or not. I had been working for President Grant, and he sent me to talk to President Hays."

"I'm certainly glad you're here. We've lost a lot of calves and cattle the last few years."

Gus stood. "We'll talk more after I do some investigation, but for now we're headed to the Roscoe place to let him know, also."

Jerrold Hawk rose and walked with them to their horses, "I'll keep quiet until you tell me better."

Gus mounted. "Thank you, sir, and I'm glad to make your acquaintance."

They rode off toward the Roscoe ranch.

As Gus and Sheriff Lacey approached the ranch, Earl Roscoe came riding out to meet them. When he saw Gus dressed in black he spoke out to Sheriff Lacey. "Did you catch our rustler, Bob?"

"Good Morning, Earl. No, not yet. This is Commodore Kelley, Earl. He has some things that you ought to know."

"Okay, I'm listening."

They pulled up, and moved the horses so that Gus and Earl were face to face. "The letter that you and Mister Hawk sent to President Hays got his attention."

Earl Roscoe smiled and said, "Well, that's good; I was about to give up."

"Things move a little slow when they have ta go clear across the country and get into the government. Anyway, I've been sent here to find out what's happenin'."

"That sounds good, but we haven't been able to get nothin' done. How do you plan to?"

"First I want to do some investigation, and I'd prefer that not everyone knew who I am or why I'm here."

"Well, just who are you?" asked Earl Roscoe.

Sheriff Lacey spoke up, "He's the new Marshall, but he don't want anyone to know it yet, because Marshall Claxton and Judge Hargrove might be in the middle of it all."

"Might be?" exclaimed Earl Roscoe, I'd bet my next calf crop on it! Them and that Rice Stanford!"

"Then I'll be able to count on your help?" asked Gus.

"You sure can, we need to put a stop to it, 'cause it's costin' us a lot of money!"

"After I find out more I'll count on you and Mister Hawk. Bob, I guess we had better get back . . . I'll ride in first by myself right down the middle of the street; maybe that'll make folks think I was out of town by myself."

Not knowing who or how many might be involved with rustling, Gus made it a point to stop in at the Gentlemen's Retreat so that he could be seen by Rice's people and others. He noticed that each time he came into the saloon, Tiny Marsh seemed to be there. After a drink and a short visit with Louise, he headed on to the boarding house.

After washing up, he went to the dining room. It was about time to close it up. Annie served Gus and sat down across from him. "You look tired, Gus."

"I guess I am, Annie, I rode out to the ranches today."

"Harve asked to leave early. I guess we know where he was headed."

"Annie, do you suppose that Rice Stanford might hire me? Since folks seem to think I'm a gunslinger, maybe I could get on the inside?"

"Gosh, Gus, I don't know, I don't think anyone knows what you do, so it could be safe to try."

"Actually, Charlie Wong knows," he said quietly.

"Why in the world did you tell him?" she asked, a little upset.

"I didn't tell him, he figured it out by my shirt."

"Your shirt?" came her puzzled response.

"Yea. He's quite a detective. He saw the badge holes in my shirt. He does Sheriff Lacey's laundry."

"Oh, I see. I don't think Charlie will say anything. He doesn't care much for Rice. Rice gave him a hard time about a year ago."

"I don't think he will either; he said he wouldn't, and that's good enough for me," said Gus.

"All right, Gus. I'll manage to say something that will cue Harve that you were asking about a job, and tell him you were turned down."

"Good. I'll make sure they know over at the Gentlemen's Retreat I was turned down. If I play it right, word will get to Rice real quick. Now, how about that walk in the moonlight?"

"As soon as dinner is over and Helen comes in to take over, I'll be ready!"

Gus sat on the front porch to wait for Annie to finish up her work. It wasn't a long wait, and when Annie appeared in the doorway, Gus stood and reached for her hand. She took his hand and said, "Why, Gus, you look absolutely dashing!"

"I don't know exactly how to take that; do you mean I look like I'm ready to run?"

"No, silly. I mean you look like a knight out of the past!"

"So, now I look old and as if I had on an iron suit!" joked Gus.

"You know I didn't mean *that*!"

He laughed and responded, "I know what you meant . . . I was a little overwhelmed by your beauty and the wonderful scent of flowers that fill the air when you are near."

"Oh, so now I wear too much perfume?" She bit her lip to keep from smiling."

"Doggone it! Let's start over. I think you are beautiful, and that you smell great! Now, let's move on. The moon won't wait for us."

"You think I'm beautiful?"

Gus paused and looked her into her eyes. "Yes, I do, whether you are here, at work, or maybe in my arms."

The thought of being in his arms excited Annie, "Oh! Really?"

"Yes, really!"

She slipped her arm in his and they walked toward the river. "Gus, thank you."

"For what?" he asked.

"For taking time to see that I have a bit of fun occasionally."

"Why, I have no idea what you mean, ma'am."

"Oh, I think you do. You know I don't have time to get out and do things, yet you cause me to take the time."

"Hey, I have an ulterior motive. I like being with you, and we're partners in skullduggery."

"Skullduggery?"

"Yes, you are helping me infiltrate a suspected ring of thieves."

"Oh, that."

"Yes, that. Don't you know it's in the interest of the United States of America?"

"So, that's the only reason we're here together?"

"No, I want to be with you, whether you help me or not." He stopped walking and turned her to face him. He took her in his arms, drew her close, and kissed her. He noticed she didn't resist and he felt her shiver.

As he held her close, she stood on her tiptoes and kissed him again. After the kiss, she smiled and said, "Okay, I believe you."

Gus' heart was racing as they walked to the river without saying anything. They arrived at the river's edge as the moon eased above the horizon and filled the scene with its golden light.

"Oh, Gus, it is beautiful. Why didn't you make me come sooner?

"You will remember that I tried."

They kissed again then stood silently watching the moon rise.

Chapter Four

Gus began to visit the Gentlemen's Retreat more often, entering into card games, and getting to know people, especially those associated with Rice Stanford.

Annie let it slip to Harve that Gus was looking for a job.

After getting friendly with Tiny Marsh, Gus was asked to visit Rice's ranch.

Not knowing exactly why he had been summoned to the ranch, Gus rode slowly through the gate, and up to the main house, constantly watching.

Rice Stanford met him at the hitching post. "Mister Kelley, get down and visit a while."

"I don't mind if I do; it's quite a ride out here."

"Yea, I like it that way . . . keeps out the riffraff."

Gus smiled, "I can agree with that."

Rice pulled out a cigar and lit it. "I understand you might be lookin' for a job."

"Yea, I thought I might hang around these parts a while."

"Kinda sweet on the bordin' house lady, I guess."

"Well, she *is* mighty nice," said Gus.

"You do know if I was to hire you, you'd have to stay here on the ranch most of the time."

"Sure, that's where the work is . . . but you would give a man a little courtin' time though, wouldn't you?"

"I reckon I would, if I hired him." said Rice.

"I've met your foreman, Blake Conway, and Tiny Marsh; they seem to be easy to get along with."

"Yea, they are good hands," he looked Gus over and said, "How are you with a gun?"

"I guess all right . . . haven't had any complaints," answered Gus.

"That tells me they weren't *able* to complain."

"Whatever you think."

"Well, I'll have Blake let you know something in a day or two."

"That sounds good to me."

Gus mounted up and rode back to town. He stopped in at the saloon, chatted with Louise, and then went to the boarding house.

Annie was behind the lobby desk. The sun shining through the window highlighted her golden hair, just as Gus had seen her on that first day. He stood for a while just looking at her, until she noticed him standing in the doorway.

"Hello, Gus. How was your ride?"

"Not sure . . . I reckon I'll get an answer in a few days. Are you still serving dinner?"

"Sure, go on in and have a seat; be there in a few minutes," said Annie.

It was late, not many customers, so Annie sat with Gus. "Well, how did you and Rice get along?"

"He seemed okay. I figger he might be lookin' for a gun hand; he quizzed me as to whether I was good with a gun or not."

"What did you tell him?"

"Actually, nothing. I phrased my answer so he could make his own deductions . . . and he did."

"Then he thinks you are a gun hand."

"I hope so . . . but I don't want him to test me."

"What do you mean, Gus?"

"I don't want one or two of his hired guns to challenge me."

"Don't you think you could take them?"

"Now that's a silly question! It would depend on the circumstance. Besides, you know what I do for a living, and I might be a little rusty. He also told me I would have to stay on the ranch."

"Oh, would that make a difference to you?"

"It might . . . some feller might come along and beat my time with you, and I wouldn't like that."

She smiled and joked. "It would have to be somebody from out of town."

"Gosh, that sounds like I might just be okay since I'm from out of town. Or is that just until a better one comes along."

"I'll tell you now, Gus, you don't have to worry." She wanted him to know how she felt about him.

Within two days, Blake Conway approached Gus as he sat with Louise in the Gentlemen's Retreat.

"Kelley, the boss wants to see you at the ranch first thing tomorrow."

"Thanks, Blake; tell him I'll be there."

"And bring your sugan and warbag."

"Will do," answered Gus as he thought, *looks like I might be employed.*

Gus readied his things to take to the ranch. He sorted and stored the things he wanted to leave at the boarding house until he could come back to town. Then he went down for an early breakfast.

Annie came to his table and sat down. "How long until I see you again?"

"I don't think it will be long. He said he gives days off. Somethin' else, do you have a place at your house where I can store the stuff I don't plan to take?"

"Gus, did you forget . . . this *is* my house."

"Sorry, I wasn't thinkin'. I was afraid if I kept the room to store it in, Harve might tell Rice . . . then I might have to stand behind my inference that I'm a gun for hire."

"You can leave your things in my room; I have three rooms and plenty of storage areas."

"Okay, you keep Harve busy with the kitchen, and I'll move my things into your room, and you can put them wherever you have a space. Oh, and thank you!"

'You're welcome. I'll be up before you leave. The crowd is coming in and Harve will be busy."

"What about servin'?" asked Gus.

"This is Helen's day to come in; she is back in the kitchen so they won't miss me."

Gus was moving the last of his things, mostly paperwork, into Annie's room when she walked in.

"Looks like you have it taken care of . . . I'll put it away after you leave. That sounds so final. 'After you leave'."

Gus saw tears well up in her eyes. "It's not final; I promise to be back." He reached out and pulled her close, held her gently, and kissed her. "I better go before . . . I . . . I'm late."

At the livery, Gus saddled his horse and was tying on his bags and sugan, when Paul Larkin, the livery owner approached. "Looks like you might be leavin'."

"Yes, sir. I got a job out at Rice Stanford's ranch."

"I reckon you won't be back then," said Paul Larkin.

"What do you mean?" asked Gus.

"Well, most that goes to Rice's either stays on or just don't come back."

"I see. I'll keep that in mind. Thank you, Paul."

Gus was hired by Rice and was immediately shown, by map, how to go to a line camp up in a north pasture to watch the cattle until he was called back.

After Gus had left, Rice assigned Farley Beck to take his old military glasses and ride that area unseen each day to see what Gus would do while he was alone.

When Gus arrived at the line camp, he decided to check it out before unloading his gear. He stepped down and put the reins in the ring on the post and tried the door. It didn't give. He took the map that Rice had given him to make sure he was at the right camp. He determined that he was at the right camp. As he folded the map to put it away, he saw writing on the back side. *The key is hanging on the underside of the rain barrel stand.*

"Never ran into anything like that before. Wonder what could be so important that it has to be locked up", he mumbled. "Guess if you have a bunch of thieves around you gotta be careful!"

After retrieving the key, he let himself in. He stood in the doorway and couldn't help being impressed. The interior of the cabin was as plush as the finest ranch house. "Rice must'a spent a lot of money to make this place look like this," he mumbled.

Looking around, he saw a gun cabinet with rifles, shotguns and cleaning equipment. There was a nice kitchen with everything a man would want for cooking. That is when he saw the sign. *This place had better look like it does now when you leave. Rice.*

Gus smiled and continued to survey the cabin. "Just a guess, but I bet Rice comes up here fairly often," he said aloud.

He unloaded his sugan and warbag, eased out his gun belt and Colt 44-40, and placed them on the table. *I guess a good cleanin' will be in order once I get settled.*

He stepped outside to tend to his horse, Pepper. He led him through the gate into the small shed where he gave him feed and hay and rubbed him down.

After he finished, he was walking to the gate when a flash from the distance caught his eye. "Now what'a you suppose that was?" He said aloud. He didn't let on he had seen anything out of the ordinary and walked back to the front of the cabin. He took a bucket that was hanging by the rain barrel and pretended to fill it, while he scanned the horizon. Nothing moved, so he went inside and quickly got his glasses and stood as close to the window as he could without being seen from outside.

In a few minutes, he saw the flash again. "Well, there you go! Rice has a man with glasses watchin' me. You'll learn to not look into the sun with your glasses; they send a nice message to the one you're spyin' on." He smiled, "Okay, if it's a show you want, Mister Stanford, a show you'll get," he mused.

Gus went out to the wood pile and began to cut wood and stack it. He worked until the sun sank into the hills behind the cabin, then he went inside.

Farley Beck rode into headquarters well after dark and reported to Rice. "Mister Stanford, looks like he might be a good hand; he chopped more wood before he went in for the night."

"Chopped more wood, did he? Well, go back in the mornin' and keep an eye on him."

"Yes, sir, I'll be there a'fore sunrise."

Before he left, Farley turned to Rice, "Mister Stanford, what's he supposed to be doin'?"

"Just let me know if he examines the cattle close, or if he just checks their condition. I'll ride out in a day or two after you report in the morning and quiz him to see if he has anything to say about the condition of the stock, or if he wonders about the different brands. If we check him out now, maybe we can determine if he's anything but what he says he is."

"All right; I'll be there a'fore he wakes up in the mornin'."

Gus was up before dawn, and fixed his breakfast. When he had finished cleaning up, he went out and saddled his horse. "Well, Pepper, we seem to be watched . . . don't know why, but I suspect he wants to know if I'm goin' to be nosey or will I make a good hand. I suppose I should make a serious effort to just be a cowboy out here to make sure the cattle are in good shape."

Gus rode the pasture out and then saw a cow that appeared to be tangled in something. On closer inspection Gus found her tangled in a short section of bailing wire left over from one of those new bailing machines invented by Charles Withington back in 1872.

"Pepper, this feller Rice Stanford must have one of the new hay bailers. I've seen a couple back east, but never this far west. Let's get this cow back to camp and see if I can do somethin' with that cut on her leg."

He untangled her, herded her back to the camp and put her in one of the stalls, then gave her hay. "You work on that hay while I see if you have much damage. Eat all you want 'cause I see now that the barn is full of bales."

Gus washed the cow's leg, dusted it with sulfur powder, and while he was working on her, his thoughts came pretty quick. *If all the pastures have as many cattle as this one does, I guess that's why he has all this new equipment for storin' hay, 'cause they sure would use up all the grass pretty quick.*

Having watched Gus most of the day, Farley Beck eased back against a tree to rest awhile, but because of his long days and short nights, he drifted off to sleep. When he awoke, Gus was riding up.

Gus smiled, "Hello Farley. Guess you been ridin' all day. You must be tired. Why don't you come over to the cabin; its real close, and I got supper started."

"Yea, I was a little tired, just takin' a minute to get the wrinkles out," replied Farley, figuring that sounded like a good excuse.

"Ridin' will do that," agreed Gus. "Anyway, why don't you ride on down, and we'll eat."

"I guess it wouldn't hurt. Chow at the ranch 'ud be gone by the time I got there."

They rode to the cabin as the sky turned to red and gold; flights of birds were hurrying toward the trees. The wind had died and a shaft of smoke rose straight up from the chimney of the cabin.

"Do you plan to go back tonight? Gus asked.

"Spect I'd better, right after I eat . . . and I sure do thank you for askin' me to supper."

Gus had cooked plenty thinking he could have the rest tomorrow, so there was enough food for both. "You ride much at night, Farley? Gus asked.

"Sometimes. I know the trails around here purdy good."

They took their time eating, and then Gus said, "I'll take care of my horse, you go ahead and finish eatin'."

"I could help you clean up," said Farley.

"Naw, you go ahead, I'll take care of that . . . you got a long way to ride."

Gus was brushing Pepper and watching the cabin. Soon Farley mounted up, hollered a 'thanks' to Gus as he rode on toward the ranch house.

Gus smiled and kept brushing. "Well, Pepper, do you think we made a good impression on Farley? If we did, I'm sure his boss'll be impressed too."

Chapter Five

The morning was ablaze with a beautiful sunrise Gus took a deep breath, stretched his arms and sighed. He watched a squirrel for a while, finished drinking his coffee, and then pondered the question, *I wonder what Rice thought when Farley came in too late to report.*

At the ranch after breakfast, Farley went into the main house. "Mister Stanford, I got in too late to come by last night."

"I noticed, and just why was that?" Rice asked.

"Well, Commodore rode up on me before I knew it and asked me to eat supper. I wanted to be polite and maybe even get to know more about him, so I stayed and we talked."

"About what?"

"About ranchin', mostly. Not much else."

"What all did he do?"

"He just rode around like he was lookin' at the condition of the cattle, and he found an old cow tangled in haywire and took her in and doctored her."

"So he didn't examine brands and such."

"No, sir; and he seemed to be a real nice hand. He told me about pushin' cattle up the trails and of spendin' time in cabins that sure weren't near as nice as that one."

"Maybe he isn't here to check to see if the cattle are stolen," he mused, "Okay, since you got acquainted with him, you can go with him over to the Hampton place. I got a bunch of cattle over there that the brands gotta be run," said Rice.

"What'a you think he'll say about that?" Farley asked.

"That's what I want to find out. Everybody in town thinks my cattle are all stolen, so I want to know if he's been talkin' to somebody and is here to try to see if it's true.   You get a couple of the boys, and tell 'em all I bought all them cows over in Farmington, and they were already branded, so we're going to run them to my brand. Here's what I want it to look like," Rice handed a paper with the brand showing how the final brand would look when they finished running it. "Tell 'em it's one of my registered brands."

"All right, sir. Are you goin' out to the cabin before you want me to come?" Farley asked.

"Yea. Give a few hours before you come out to the cabin. Saddle up my horse for me . . . I'll be out there in a while. I'm sendin' a couple of wagons of hay to the Hampton, too; I imagine the grass is about gone."

LaRice, Rice Stanford's daughter, stepped into the room, "Daddy, are you going to ride this morning? If you are I'd like to ride with you."

"Well, dear, it *is* business . . . but I guess it will be all right."

"Thank you, Daddy, I'm all ready to go, Sony is saddled and ready, too."

"Okay, we'll leave in a few minutes."

Rice and his daughter rode toward the pasture with the cabin, "Where are we going, Daddy?" LaRice asked.

"Out to the east pasture cabin."

"Oh, good, I love that cabin, it's so homey!"

When they reached the cabin, Gus was working on the roof. "Well, a good mornin' to the Stanfords."

LaRice looked close, "Oh, it's Mister Kelley!"

"You know this man?" Rice asked somewhat surprised.

"Yes, Daddy, He danced with me at the church when none of the boys asked."

"Is that so?" said Rice.

"Mister Stanford, you and LaRice go on inside; there's hot coffee on the stove. I've finished repairs on the roof, so I'll be right down."

As Rice and his daughter went inside, she said, "Isn't he a nice man, Daddy?"

"I guess so," replied Rice as he considered maybe he had Gus figured wrong.

Gus brushed his boots on the mat outside the door and went in. "Did you folks find the coffee all right?"

"We did and it's good."

"How are you this morning, LaRice?"

Rice was impressed that Gus knew how to pronounce his daughter's name.

"I'm fine, and I enjoyed the ride here this morning," she replied.

"Did you folks have breakfast? I can fix something real quick. The beans are still hot, and I sliced ham a while ago for lunch."

"No, thank you, Gus, We ate before we left; the coffee is plenty and besides, several of the boys will be here shortly for a job in another place."

As Gus poured himself a cup of coffee, he was thinking, *Havin' brought his daughter, and assignin' me to a new job, maybe he's sold on my bein' a good hand.*

Rice began telling Gus about the job he had for him. "I bought some cattle a while back, and I'm sending some of the boys over there. I want you to go with them . . . they'll tell you what we need to do when you get there."

"All right, Mister Stanford; sounds good. LaRice, I enjoyed the dance the other night, and I'm glad that it gave me a chance to meet you."

"Thank you Mister Kelley; it was nice."

Rice stood and moved toward the door, "We were out for a ride, Gus; we're gonna get back to it. We'll see you when the job is finished. You can come on back to headquarters with the others then."

As Rice Stanford and his daughter left, Gus leaned against the door frame watching them ride away. As he stood there, three riders came from the trail to headquarters and rode up to the hitching post.

"Hello, Farley. You fellers get down and have some coffee. It's on the stove."

"Howdy, Gus. I guess you ain't met these hands yet. This here's Noble Temple," He referred to the tall lanky man with a front tooth missing and a heavy beard."

"Glad to meet you, Noble," said Gus

Farley turned to the other man, "And this here's Chuck Parnell."

Gus extended his hand, "Gad to meet you too, Chuck. My name is Commodore Kelley, but call me Gus. You fellers get ready for lots of eats later this evening, I been cookin' a big chunk of beef all day, and if we are leavin' in the mornin' and won't be back, we better eat all we can."

Later, Farley turned to the barrel and drew water into the pan to wash. "I been workin' since four thirty this morning, and I'm shore glad we don't have to ride to the Hampton right now. I'm all tuckered out."

Gus turned and took another look at Chuck Parnell. *I'm sure I've seen this one somewhere before . . . I just can't place where, or when.*

Chuck Parnell was tall, had a dark complexion, and a deep scar over his left eye brow.

After they ate supper that evening, the three of them sat out where they could watch the sun go down and drink coffee.

Gus still had not remembered where he might have seen Chuck Parnell before, "Chuck, you been with Rice long?" Gus asked.

"Oh, I'd say about a year. I came here from Tulsa, Oklahoma."

Gus had hoped that he would say where he came from, but that didn't seem to help his memory.

"I was in Oklahoma, but that was a long time ago. I came from far east Virginia, and I kinda fell in love with this part of the country.

"What he means is he fell in love with a little blonde that owns the boardin' house!" said Farley.

"Well, she *is* pretty nice."

Next morning when the four, Farley Beck, Nobel Temple, Chuck Parnell, and Gus arrived at the Hampton, Gus was surprised by the number of cattle that covered the whole place. "They've just about eaten all the grass, and what they haven't eaten, they have stomped into the ground!"

Farley agreed. "It does look purdy bad, don't it! I reckon that's why the boss is sendin' some wagons of hay up here. They should be here by this afternoon, and when they get here, we'll spread the hay close so the cattle will be close to work on."

Gus stepped down and stood in the shade of a tree, "Now, what is it we're supposed to do with these cattle?"

Farley joined Gus in the shade, "Well, the boss said he bought these cattle in Farmington, New Mexico, and the old boy he got 'em from was from Texas, and his brand was a TX. He said that this brand," Farley pull out the paper that Rice Stanford had given him and showed it to Gus, "is what he wanted it changed to, box IX, 'cause he had this brand registered in his name. See here how that TX can be changed by puttin' a box around it?"

"Dang, Farley, that don't sound legal! Has Rice got a bill of sale on these cattle? If he does, he doesn't have to rebrand 'em."

"That's what he wants to do, and they are his cattle."

As a lawman, Gus couldn't help being suspicious. *When I think about it, there's nothin' illegal about changin' brands on your own cattle . . . if they are your cattle.*

As the wagons arrived the hay was spread nearby and a fire was built to heat the running iron. The work ran well into the night. Gus carefully observed every move and kept count of the cattle on which the brand had been changed.

When the work was completed, Farley walked over to where Gus had sat down. "Well, that took longer than we thought. Looks like we'll have to camp here and go in the morning."

Gus smiled at Farley. "You got food in your pocket, Farley?"

"Nope, but they brought food in the wagons, and Noble is a good cook! They also brought bedding for all of us. I guess Mister Stanford knew it would take a long time. Let's you and me get a good cookin' fire goin' and find a good place to bed down for the night."

When the men had finished eating, the others picked up their saddles that they had been leaning on and moved away from the fire to find a place to sleep. Farley and Gus still sat by the fire.

"Farley, how long did you say you have worked for Rice?"

"I didn't. I been working for Rice for three years. When I came to Sykesville I'd been on the run. I got in a little trouble in Arizona and Rice took care of it, so I been workin' for him ever since."

Gus sat starring into the fire; he ran all the things that had taken place today through his mind. *I still can't place this Chuck Parnell . . . I know I've seen him somewhere.*

When it got quiet, Farley felt the need to speak up. "You said you came from Virginia; what did you do there?"

"Oh, I had some livestock and I even did a little farmin."

"How come you came out this far west?"

Gus didn't answer right away, and then, "It just seemed the right thing to do. My brother came out here somewhere, and I thought I might run into him sometime."

"You don't know where he is?"

"Naw, we never really got along. Tell me, Farley, have all these hands been in trouble?"

"Most of 'em, why?"

"Oh I just wondered. You said you had, and usually people that hadn't been in trouble before don't like workn' with those that had."

Farley looked at Gus, "You never been on the other side of the law?"

Gus, thinking about what he might have done today said, "Yea, Farley, I guess I have."

Farley stood and moved to his bed.

When Gus lay down on his bedding, he had trouble going to sleep because of all the events of the day, plus trying to remember where he had come across Chuck Parnell.

Next morning Gus rose early, rolled his bedding, washed up, and was ready for breakfast. Noble Temple handed Gus a plate of bacon and eggs. "You fellers always eat like this when you're out on the range?" Gus asked.

"The boss thinks a man's gotta have a good breakfast to get the work done."

Chuck Parnell walked up with his plate and cup and sat beside Gus. "Now you see why some of us been workin' here so long."

"I could sure get used to this," said Gus, taking a bit of his food. Then he got quiet, racking his brain trying to think where he had seen that face.

The group returned to headquarters, and Gus went in to talk to Rice Stanford. "If you don't mind, I'd like to go into town for the weekend, unless there is something I need to do before then."

Rice moved to a small table by his overstuffed leather chair and asked, "Want to see Miss Shaw pretty bad, huh?"

"It would be kinda nice. When I left she asked me to go to church with her Sunday, if that's all right."

"Why, that would be nice. It would be good for one of my hands to be seen in church by townsfolk. They think I only hire criminals. By the way, Farley was quite impressed with your work."

"I appreciate that. I try to give my best," said Gus, as he wondered when Farley had a chance to report on him.

"Would you like a drink before you go?" Rice poured one drink, and was about to pour another.

"I think I'll pass this mornin'. It's still a bit early for me."

Rice raised his drink as a salute. "Well, give Miss Shaw my regards."

"I will, sir." Gus turned and left.

Rice watched through the window as Gus rode off toward town, and then he turned and asked his maid to get Blake Conway, his foreman, to come in.

"You wanted to see me, Boss?"

"Yes, pour yourself one while we talk. Did you have a chance to talk to Nobel and Chuck about Gus?"

"Yea, and Farley too, but nothin' much came of it. Only thing, he wondered if it was legal, and why we were goin' to all the trouble changing brands if you had a bill of sale, 'cause then it wouldn't be necessary."

"Do you think he would be all right to take on as a regular hand?"

Blake Conway sipped on his drink, "I don't know, Farley said he had been outside the law before."

"Wonder how far outside the law."

"I don't know, but they said he was at ease when Farley told him to not worry, you would take care of it."

Rice turned on his heels and shouted "Farley told him that?"

"Well, he didn't say you would, exactly, he said Judge Hargrove could."

"What did he say to that?" asked Rice.

"I guess he thought it was all right, he worked hard after that, they said."

"I don't want him to think we work outside the law. Send Tiny into town to keep an eye on what he does and where he goes and report back to me."

Gus rode directly to the livery stables, and left Pepper with Paul Larkin, the owner. "Take good care of him Paul; we rode in purty fast."

"I'll give him a good rub and feed him some grain, too."

"Thanks, I'll probably pick him up Sunday."

Gus walked to the boarding house, by-passing the Gentlemen's Retreat, and walked through the opened door where he saw Helen Thomas behind the desk. "Annie around, Helen?"

"Hello, Gus. She's in her room. She just went up."

Gus bounded up the steps, taking them two at a time. His boots made so much noise that Annie opened her door and stepped out into the hall to see what was going on. Gus hit the top just as she stepped out, and he grabbed her in his arms and swung her around. "Did you miss me?" he asked.

"Yes, I did . . . now, what was your name?" she joked.

He pulled her close again and kissed her, "Now do you remember me?"

She faked a puzzled look, "Weren't you with that bunch that passed through last fall?"

"Okay, enough, or I'll spread rumors on you out at Rice's, and then you'll be sorry," He joked.

"How did that go, Gus?" she asked seriously.

"Well, I have my suspicions, but I have no solid proof. Would you have someone ask Sheriff Lacey to meet me here? I don't want us to be seen together if I can help it. I'm sure I'm being watched."

"You mean, now?"

"Yes if you don't mind. As soon as I get that out of the way, I have nothin' 'till Sunday night."

"Nothing? So that's what I am to you!"

"I just meant I wouldn't have anything *but* you!"

"That's more like it, I'll tell Jessup to get him to come right away."

In the meeting with Sheriff Lacey, Gus told him of the brand changing, and that he didn't know if Rice actually had a bill of sale for the cattle or not. "He does have the brand that we change to, registered to his name, because I saw it. I couldn't figger out why change the brand if he had a bill of sale? He even had a drawin' of how to change the brand."

Sheriff Lacey rubbed his chin, "He's a hard man to understand. What do you think is next?"

"I'm not sure . . . he may have more tests for me."

"Okay, Gus. Keep me informed."

"Will do, but before you go, I'd like to borrow that colt of yours? I need to do some business over close to San Angelo, and be back in time to go to church in the mornin'. Think he can stand up to a good fast ride?"

"Why, shore. Your horse gone lame?"

"Naw, I just don't want Pepper to be out of the livery, so folks won't know I'm gone for a while."

"Yeah, I understand." Sheriff Lacey left, and went to the dining room for coffee and a piece of pie to make it seem that is why he came to the boarding house. After serving the sheriff, Annie went back up to her room.

When she came through the door, Gus asked if any of Rice's men had *just happened* to drift into the boarding house.

"No. Would you like to have talked to them too?"

"Now don't get sassy, missy. I'll take you over my knee. Dang, Annie, I hate being away from you like I have been."

"I hate it too, Gus, but it's your job, and I understand."

"Yea, but this is the part I don't like! I've got to ride over by San Angelo to talk to a man."

56

"Tonight? Why on earth?"

"Yes, tonight, I'm sorry. It's tough, but that's why they call it undercover."

"Undercover? You don't really get under any covers do you?" she said coyly.

"Naw, it's what they call gettin' in with the bad guys, and makin' them think you're one of 'em."

"Do you think Rice thinks you're one of his bunch?"

"I hope so . . . if not, my goose may be cooked!"

"When do you have to go back?"

"Sunday evenin'."

"Well, at least we've got a little time to spend together, that is, if you get back tonight!"

"I gotta get back tonight. I told them that's why I came to town, because I promised you I'd go to church with you."

As they both stood up, Gus took her in his arms, "Annie, as long as I know that you are waitin' for me, I'll be quick. The Sheriff's little colt is fast and has a lot of stamina, so expect me back before you go to sleep," he pulled her close and kissed her, "By the way, save a little of that roast, 'cause I'm sure I'll be hungry." Annie threw a pillow at him as he went out the door.

Chapter Six

Gus stepped out the back door of the boarding house and hurriedly moved down the alley. He stayed close to the backs of the buildings because it wasn't totally dark.

By the time he arrived at Sheriff Lacey's pen where he kept his horses, it was dark. He lifted the latch, and as he did, he heard a soft snort from near the shed where the hay was kept. "I hear you, boy, I'm coming." The colt was black and was hard to see. He eased toward where the sound came from, and found that Sheriff Lacey had him saddled and ready to go. He took the reins and led the colt out of the pen, tightened the cinch, mounted up, and hurriedly headed toward San Angelo.

The full moon would soon be coming up, so he put on a bit more speed.

His destination was the home of David Berkshire, who had recently moved to near San Angelo to open his own law practice. When he arrived a light was shinning in the front room window. He tied the horse to the rack and stepped up on the porch. David Berkshire must have heard his steps on the porch because he opened the door about the time Gus reached it.

"Hello, David," Gus greeted.

Squinting to see in the dark, David Berkshire said, "Commodore? . . . is that you?"

"Yep," came Gus' reply.

"Come on in. What in the world are you doing in this neck of the woods?"

"Workin' as usual," said Gus.

"It's good to see you, how long has it been?" David Berkshire asked.

"I'd guess three or more years. How's Genevieve?"

"She's doing fine . . . I'm sure glad to see you. I have coffee on the stove, want a cup?"

"You bet I do, and tell her hello for me. I need to talk as I drink 'cause I've gotta get back to Sykesville, shortly. I've been appointed Marshall for this district because of trouble with cattle rustling, as well as trouble with the Court."

"Problems with the Court?"

"Yes, maybe. They can't get convictions when they arrest people. President Hayes' Attorney General, Charles Bevins, has appointed you to take over the Court in this district. I have the appointment letter, and I'm here to tell you, and to help you get settled into that position. I also think that the former Marshall could be in with the whole organization, but his time was out when my term started. I haven't let anyone know that the change is coming, because I needed to find out what exactly is going on. I've hired on with the man that is probably behind the problems but haven't enough evidence yet."

"My, Gus. That's a lot to take in! I'd planned to start a practice here in San Angelo."

"Sykesville is a nice town, David, and it may not last long if the railroad passes it by. But I think the trouble lies there. Once we've sorted things all out, you can take over. Think about who you would like for clerk and others you'll need, and I'll get with you as soon as this business is straightened out. I just wanted to let you know of your appointment, and I will let you know when I get to the bottom of it all."

"Gus, you're still the same." Berkshire said as he waved his arms around. "Like a mighty whirlwind, you swoop in and before you realize it, you're gone. Okay, let me know. I'll be here."

Gus stood to leave. "I will, but right now I have to get back. Only the Sheriff and Miss Annie Shaw know I'm gone."

David Berkshire smiled at Gus, "Oh, a Miss, is it?"

Gus grinned as he walked toward the door. "Yeah. I'll see you later."

Gus rode the mustang colt hard. He stopped a couple of times to rest the horse and still made it in time for church.

Gus quickly washed, changed clothes, combed his hair and moved into the hallway just as Annie opened her door. "I didn't think you were back yet."

"I told you I would be. When are you going to be convinced that I'm a man of my word?"

"Well, you may have proved it this morning," she answered as she moved to the steps, "By the way, you look nice."

"Well, thank you. You see . . . you can be nice when you try."

After the main church service, the congregation gathered for the monthly pot-luck meal. While they were enjoying the food and conversation, Gus decided it was a good time to tell Annie that he would be expected to drop into the Gentlemen's Retreat before returning to Rice's ranch.

"Why do you feel you must go to *that place*?"

"I want them to think I'm truly riding for the brand. Going to the hub of their information gathering place should do that."

"I guess so . . . but I don't like your having to go there."

"Are you a little jealous of Louise?" he chided.

"Louise Webber never saw the day that I would be jealous of anything that would look at her twice!"

"Well you don't have to worry. I'm goin' to talk to the hands. Maybe I can get a bit of information if I listen. Look, it will only be for a while, and then I can be with you more."

"Well, okay, but I don't like it!" she pouted.

He reached over and kissed her on the cheek.

Her face turned a fiery red. "Don't do that here! What will people think?"

"And here I thought you liked giving people something to talk about."

"I just don't want them to think I'm the same caliber as Louise Webber," she whispered.

"Okay, I'm sorry I embarrassed you, but what do you think these folks will say when I visit the Gentlemen's Retreat? Will you not want me to come visit you?"

"Yes I do!" She giggled and said, "You can come in by the back door."

"I get it; it's okay to visit as long as I don't let anyone see me."

She turned toward him, "No, I want you to visit, and I want you to come in the front door."

He looked deep into her eyes and whispered, "I want to come in your front door all right, and I want to hold you and kiss you, right now."

Annie's good friend, Betty Sue McKlesky, sitting down the table from them, said in a low voice, "You two better hold it down or the whole town will be talking tomorrow . . . sister Franks is keeping an eye on both of you," she said, rolling her eyes in the direction of the next table.

After taking Annie's lunch basket back to the boarding house, Gus and Annie walked arm and arm along the river. Occasionally Gus would find a flat rock, and would stop long enough to skip it across the river.

As he walked her back to the boarding house, Annie asked, "Gus, how long do you think you will have to be part of this gang of thieves?"

"Now, Annie, I don't know for sure they are thieves. Anyway, It shouldn't take too much longer . . . I expect I'll be called upon to go on the next expedition so they can watch me. Who knows, I may have to rustle some cattle."

He ushered her inside and said, "I'll see you in a few days."

Gus stepped out the front door and headed to the saloon. Before he entered, he looked over the swinging doors to see if the men he wanted to impress were inside. Near the back, a table of four men played cards. Gus moved toward them.

Farley noticed Gus first. "Hey, Gus, come on back. Do you play cards?"

"No, Farley, I don't play 'cause I'm not too good; maybe some other time. Right now I'll just watch."

Gus watched them play a while, and then he moved to the next table where Louise Webber held off two guys that had had too much to drink. Gus told them, "You boys need to go home; you've had a little too much to drink."

From the table he had just left came the words, "Let 'em alone, Kelley. They're just having a little fun. They're harmless."

When Gus turned, he saw it was Chuck Parnell who had called to him. At that moment, Gus remembered where he had seen Chuck Parnell! *Bartles Town, Oklahoma. I was in the blacksmith shop when he robbed the store, and he shot a man as he came out. He never saw me, he was in such a hurry.*

Gus watched over Louise's shoulder, always keeping an eye on Chuck. It wasn't long before Chuck pitched his cards on the table and shoved his chair back hard enough to flip it over backward, and then he walked out the back door. Gus followed.

As Gus stepped out the back door, Chuck turned quickly as he heard the door close behind him.

Chuck's hand relaxed when he saw it was Gus, "What do want, Kelley."

"I was wondering if a gunman's conscience ever bothered him when he murdered in cold blood."

"What'a you mean?"

Wanting to provoke him more, Gus turned, and started to go back inside. "Don't turn your back on me," shouted Chuck Parnell. "What'd you mean by that?"

As Chuck Parnell asked the question, Gus heard the slap of leather. As always, an agitated man shoots too quickly, and his bullet went into the ground at Gus' feet; but Gus was drawing at the sound of

Chuck slapping his holster, and when he fired, it was so close to the same time that it sounded as one shot. Chuck Parnell went down.

Gus walked to where Chuck had fallen and slipped Chuck's gun back into his holster and stood over him.

The back door to the saloon burst open and a crowd flowed out into the yard.

Seeing that Chuck had fallen and his gun was still in its holster, a man shouted, "He done murdered Chuck Parnell, quick call the Sheriff!"

Gus holstered his gun and turned to the crowd, "I didn't murder anybody, he drew first!"

Nobel Temple moved up beside Gus, "It don't look like self defense . . . he didn't even get his gun out!"

"I can't help it if he's slow, when I shot him his gun dropped back into his holster! Just smell his gun; you can tell it's been fired."

Sheriff Lacey was making his way through the crowd, "Move out of the way . . . Let me through . . . what's going on here?"

"Kelley done murdered Chuck Parnell!"

Sheriff Lacey turned to the crowd, waved his hand, and said, "Break it up, I'll take care of this, you folks go on back inside."

Sheriff handcuffed Gus and took him to the jail.

After they reached the Sheriff's office, he removed the handcuffs and asked, "What in the world is goin' on Gus?"

"Well, Bob, Chuck Parnell . . . by the way his name on the wanted posters is Charles Partin . . . shot a man right in front of me while he was running from a holdup in a store in Bartles Town, Oklahoma. He didn't see me, and he never was caught. When I first saw him here I knew I'd seen him somewhere, and it just came to me tonight."

Sherriff Lacey began shuffling through the wanted posters on his desk while they talked, "Gus, I know he was wanted, but how come you shot him in cold blood?"

"I didn't, Bob; he pulled his gun and shot while I was walkin' away, nearly shot me in the back! I guess he had a hair trigger on his gun, 'cause he shot right into the ground."

"Well, what about his gun still in the holster?"

"I put it back in there to get the results that I got."

"You mean you wanted them to think you just shot him?"

"Yep, that's about it. I saw a chance to get involved in the law, at least the law here in Sykesville, and maybe we can get to the heart of the problems here."

The Sheriff scratched his head and rubbed this chin.

"You plannin' on Rice to get you straight with me."

"That's about it," said Gus.

"What if they find you guilty?"

"Look, Bob, The Hargrove court is not legal."

"What'd you mean, ain't legal?"

"I've already given Judge David Berkshire his letter of appointment by the Attorney General. He's in San Angelo, and you can contact him if it doesn't go like I'm plannin'."

"What about Marshall Claxton?"

"This is purty much your play. Claxton should stay to the side of this shootin'. If he tries to interfere, tell him it's your jurisdiction."

"Seems to me, Gus, you got this planned out purty good."

"It all happened pretty quickly, but I sure hope so, Bob. I guess you had better put me in a cell before someone walks in on us. Oh, and if you find that poster you'll see Parnell is wanted dead or alive! He's killed more than once!"

"All right, I guess that lets you off the hook, since he was wanted dead or alive. You sure you want to go through a trial?"

"It's the only way we can see if the wheels of justice are stopped or just need greasin'."

What if Rice really liked this Chuck Parnell, and he lets you get convicted?"

"I reckon, then, I'll have to turn the tables on him."

"I just hope you know what you're doin'"

"Keep the poster to yourself, and if we run into any problems, the judge can be convinced with that, and the fact that he will be fired and maybe locked up himself."

As Sheriff Lacey was locking the cell, Annie walked in, "Bob Lacey, you're not really locking him up are you?"

"Well, ma'am, he shot a man in cold blood!"

"Gus laughed. "It's all right Bob, she knows."

Sheriff Lacey unlocked the cell so Annie could go in. "It's all his idea, Annie, I sure do hope it works."

"Oh, Gus, are you sure this is the way to handle this?"

"It seemed best at the time. Maybe you had better turn against me, to play it safe."

"You mean . . . ," she hesitated.

"I mean, you don't want to be around a murderer."

Sheriff Lacey spoke up, "That might be hard Gus . . . Annie usually feeds the prisoners here at the jail."

"Oh. Okay, Annie. Let Helen bring over the food, that way Rice's bunch will think you won't have anything to do with me."

"Okay, Gus, if that's the way you want it. Try to get this cleared up soon, please."

"I will, Annie, I will." He could see the worry in her face.

It was four days before Judge Winston Hargrove decided to hear Gus' case. "All right, let's get this hearing underway. Let's see, now . . . the first witness is . . . Farley Beck. Farley, do you swear to tell the whole truth?"

"I do your honor."

"Well, sit down, and tell your story."

"Well, I guess I was out the back door of the Gentlemen's Retreat purty quick. I seen Gus . . . er . . . Mister Kelley, a standing over ole Chuck, who was just layin' there on the ground. His gun was in his holster, and it looked like he shot Chuck in cold blood, but Gus said it warn't, that Chuck was too slow and his gun just slid back in the holster. He told me to smell Chuck's gun, and I could tell he shot it."

The Judge interrupted, "Well, did it smell like he fired it?"

"I reckon it did Judge, I ain't smelled many guns, shot or not!"

"All right, Farley, you can step down," addressing those in the courtroom, the Judge continued, "I want to ask right now, did anybody in here actually see Mister Kelley shoot this feller? If any of you lie, you just might wind up in jail yourself!" The Judge waited for an answer, none came. "Next witness, Nobel Temple. Do you swear the same as Farley?"

"Yes sir, I do," said Nobel.

A brief pause followed. "Well . . . we're waiting for your story," said Judge Winston Hargrove.

Nobel lowered his head and said, "Judge, now that I think about it, what Farley said was what I seen too."

Marshall Wade Claxton sat in the court room listening to the testimony, but didn't try to participate.

When Farley and Nobel had testified, Judge Hargrove asked Gus if he had anything to say.

"Yes, your honor. I shot him in self defense!"

Judge Hargrove asked, "What about his gun still in his holster?"

"He made his play first, but he was too slow. When I shot him, his gun hadn't cleared his holster and it dropped back in," insisted Gus."

"Doesn't that sound a bit far-fetched? Asked the Judge?"

"Well, sir," said Gus, "That's the way it happened. When he started to draw on me, I was just a lot faster than he was."

As Gus was speaking, Rice Stanford entered the courtroom, and stood by the back door.

Judge Hargrove, noticing Rice, looked around the room then turned back to Gus, "Your story sounds plausible to me, and Farley did say his gun might have smelled like it had been fired . . . Commodore Kelley, I find you not guilty. Case dismissed," he said loudly.

The level of conversation in the courtroom rose considerably. One statement, louder than most others, was, "Well it's happened again! No crook's ever gonna to be convicted in this town!"

Gus sat quietly thinking, *shoot, that doesn't help at all; legally it was okay . . . but it didn't help my investigation!*

Chapter Seven

Gus, a free man again, made his way to the Gentlemen's Retreat. When he walked in, a cheer went up from the crowd. Then Louise came over to Gus, slipped her arm into his and said, "Belly up to the bar, Gus, the drinks are on me. I never cared much for old Chuck anyway."

There wasn't much Gus could say; he just stepped up to the bar and took the drink that the bartender placed before him.

"Why, thank you, Louise" he said lifting his glass in salute to her.

"Sure, Gus. I think you've earned it!"

Tiny Marsh stepped up beside Gus and said, "The Boss wants you to stop by the headquarters when you get to the ranch tonight."

"Okay, Tiny, will do."

"Me and Farley are headin' back now."

As Farley came by Gus, he stopped and said quietly, "Gus, watch out for James Cooksey. He's been at the east line shack for a couple of months and has been real close to Chuck Parnell since they come here. Anyway, he's the one with the vest and grey hat."

"Thanks, Farley. I'll keep an eye on him."

Gus stayed at the bar for a while then decided that most all the hands had gone back to the ranch, so he left.

As he walked to his horse, he heard someone call his name from the front of the saloon . . . it was James Cooksey. "Hey you . . . Kelley . . . they tell me you didn't give Chuck an even chance and shot him down in cold blood!"

"Whoever told you that was sadly mistaken; he was just slow!" Gus turned to walk to his horse.

"Don't walk away from me when I'm talkin' to you." He pulled his gun and fired at Gus.

Gus had heard his action and was turning when the shot hit him in the back of the shoulder and turned him around to face James Cooksey. As he turned, his gun blazed before he dropped to his knees, and James Cooksey folded, falling on his face in the sand.

Several men had followed Cooksey out of the saloon and had seen the whole play. One of the men shook his head and said, "I'd never thought James Cooksey would'a shot nobody in the back like that."

Gus was completely out now, and was losing blood. Sheriff Lacey had been making his rounds when it all began and had also witnessed the whole thing. He quickly came to Gus' aid.

Not realizing that Gus was unconscious, he said, "Gus, you're not gonna lay there all night, are you?"

When Gus didn't move Sheriff Lacey yelled, "Somebody help me git him to the doctor's house!"

When Annie saw them carrying Gus, she ran to his side. Sheriff Lacey said, "He's all right Annie, but he is losing blood and Doc can stop it."

"Get him to the boarding house, Bob, it's closer! I can take care of him there," Annie ordered.

They placed Gus on a bed in a room on the first floor, and Annie quickly began to dress his wound.

Doctor Parsons finally arrived. He told Annie the bullet went clear through and that she had done just fine. As he put on his hat he said, "I couldn't a done better myself . . . I'll come by later."

Hours passed. Annie never left his side but had gone to sleep leaning on his bed. He stirred slightly and when he opened his eyes, he could see Annie leaning by his side. He reached out and lightly stroked her hair. She woke and took his hand in hers, "I thought you were dead when they brought you here."

"I guess I was, 'cause I don't remember it."

She smiled and said, "Don't you know better than to get into a gunfight?"

"I don't recall havin' much choice. Annie, I'm cold."

"I'll get someone to bring some coffee; do you think you can drink it?"

"You bet I can try. Did it get cold out? I'm freezin'"

"No, Gus, you were in pretty bad shape. You lost a lot of blood!" she responded as she wiped sweat from his brow.

Helen Thomas' brother, who worked some nights, brought in coffee and cups. Annie said, "Just put it on the table, Burt. I think he has passed out again. Better see if Doc Parsons can come now." Burt hurriedly left the room.

Annie felt Gus' head, "He's burning up, I don't see how he could be cold." As she spoke she lifted the covers back and slipped in beside Gus, moving close to him. Soon he stopped shaking and the muscles that had been so tight began to relax. She got up when Doc Parsons arrived.

"He was shaking and said he was cold, Doc. I didn't know what else to do!"

He smiled. "Annie, that's about all you could do. Just let me examine that wound again, and you can get right back in there to keep him warm."

Gus was propped up with pillows so he would stay on his side, opposite the wound in his shoulder.

"Annie that shoulder still looks good. You did a good job of cleaning it when they brought him in. I reckon he'll be up and around 'fore long . . . he's pretty strong. You can get back in there now, and keep him warm. I'll check on him tomorrow."

Doctor Parsons left, and Annie slipped in beside him.

Later, Annie woke up to an, "OH! OH! OH!"

She had her back to him, but turned to face him asking, "What is it Gus?"

"I wondered who was in bed with me, and when I went to put my arm around you, it hurt like the dickens!"

"Oh! So you wondered who was in bed with you, did you? And you were still willing to put your arm around whoever it was?"

"Well, I wasn't cold anymore, so I thought I would make the most of the situation."

"Commodore Kelley, it'll be a cold day in Hades before I try to keep you warm again!"

"Now, Annie, you don't really mean that do you? I really am glad you saved my life; I might have froze to death if it hadn't been for you! 'Sides, I may ask you to keep me warm the rest of our lives," he said with a sheepish grin.

"If that's a proposal the answer is NO! Not after you just the same as told me you wanted to put your arm around *whoever* might have crawled in bed with you!"

She left the room, smiling when Gus could not see her. She could hear him moaning, "Ah, Annie, come on back, I was just kiddin'." She proceeded to get breakfast.

When Annie reached the lobby, Rice Stanford was standing there, having just come through the door.

"Well, good morning, Mister Stanford. Why don't you go right in and sit wherever you please. Harve has a good hot breakfast all ready."

"Thank you, Miss Shaw, I would like to see my employee, Mister Kelley, first, if you don't mind, and if it is all right."

"I think it will be all right for a while. I was about to take him some coffee, and he thinks he can eat a little."

"I'll not take long, I need him to get well soon . . . he's cutting down on the number of hands I have at the ranch."

"Go ahead, Mister Stanford; he's in that first room."

A gentle knock on the door brought a soft, "Come in."

"Good morning, Mister Kelley. I thought I'd come by to see when you plan to come to work; we are kind of running short, lately.

"I'm sorry about that Mister Stanford, I'm afraid it hasn't been all my fault."

"That's true; those men were a bit unruly. Gus, when do you feel you will be able to return to the ranch?"

"I haven't seen Doc Hamilton this mornin', but I'm sure feeling better than I did last night."

"I guess this is as good a place as any to heal, because I doubt that you would be able to do much at the ranch. Take your time; I need a man of your caliber in good shape when I send him on a job."

A knock came at the door, Mister Stanford opened it. Annie came in with breakfast. "Breakfast is hot, Mister Stanford."

"Annie, it smells so good, I think I'll take you up on it. You take good care of our man," said Rice as he headed for the dining room.

"I will, Mister Stanford." Annie set the tray down and asked. "What did he have to say?"

"Not much, but he indicated that a big job was coming up and he would need a man of my 'caliber' , whatever that means, to do it. Sounds to me like he's still lookin' for a gunfighter."

"Oh, Gus, I wish this was all over, I'm afraid you are going to get hurt."

"And just what do you think happened last night?" he teased.

"Oh, you know what I mean."

"Yes, I know. What I don't know is why you won't get right back in here with me."

"Well, for one thing, your breakfast is getting cold! For another, I don't trust you *or* me. Besides, I need to get back to work."

Gus took his time to heal, and then prepared to go back to Rice Stanford's ranch. As he stepped out into the hall, he saw Annie coming. She said, "I see you're dressed for the trail this morning."

"I figgered I'd laid up long enough, and if I'm goin' to get this over with I'd better move. Thank you, Annie, for takin' care of me."

"I'm glad I had the chance to, for a little while."

"I'll ride back in as soon as I can . . . though I don't know when that will be."

After his breakfast, Gus headed down the walkway toward the livery stables. Annie watched with a tear slowly rolling down her cheek.

Paul Larkin was standing in the doorway of the livery. "Well, Paul, I hope you've taken good care of Pepper while I've been laid up."

"Good to see you up and around, Gus. Yeah, we've gotten along real well, and I expect he may have put on a pound or two."

"That's all right; he'll get a good work-out headin' out to Rice's place."

"You still plannin' to work out there, are you?"

"For just a while longer, Paul."

"Well, you be careful now, you hear."

"I will, and thanks for takin' care of Pepper."

Gus rode to the ranch, and found Rice on his front porch drinking his morning coffee. "I see you've recovered real well; I'm glad you're back. Step down and have some coffee while we talk."

Gus flipped the reins over the rack, moved to the porch, poured a cup of coffee and sat opposite Rice.

"Farley told me that you have trailed cattle several times."

"Yes, sir, a few times."

"Enough that you can do it again?" asked Rice.

Gus took a drink of his coffee and then said, "I think so. What do you have in mind?"

"Well, the reason I asked is, I've purchased a small herd of about eight hundred head up in Oklahoma, and none of my men have ever trailed a herd, so I want you to take charge and show my men how it's done. You can explain to them as you go up there."

Gus smiled. "A small herd of eight hundred, huh? I guess that sounds reasonable to me. When do you want us to go? The pastures that I've seen have almost been over grazed."

"Right away. I have pastures north of here that you haven't seen. My foreman, Blake, will show you on the way."

"I'll start getting the men ready to go. They won't mind that I'll sound like I'm a new-comer telling the old hands what to do?"

"Naw, Blake has laid it out for them and they are okay with it."

"That's good. I sure don't want to twist any tails that might get me shot."

"You won't have to worry about that. Good to have you back, Gus."

"Thank you, sir."

"You can just call me Rice."

Gus got with Blake and they parleyed with the men. He laid out the positions that each would rotate during the trail back with the herd.

"Blake, I don't know if Rice knows what all it will take to do this. We'll need 60 or 70 more horses, cause they'll be workin' hard."

"We can do that."

"Good! I guess Nobel will be doing the cookin'."

"Yep, he's already volunteered."

Gus thought a minute then said, "We can get together tonight and I'll explain each job 'cause each one of us will have a turn to ride in that spot. Some of the jobs are better than others, but each man will be expected to ride there without any bellyachin'. When we have any problems, we can give extra time on the drag and let 'em eat dust on an extra rotation."

Blake chuckled." Sounds good to me."

Gus got with Nobel to prepare the chuck wagon. "I expect each man to be responsible for his tack and his sugan, but you'll be carrying on the wagon what they are not usin'."

Noble nodded and asked, "How long do you think it'll take to get up there?"

"Well, Rice said the ranch where they are holdin' the cattle is just over into Oklahoma . . . I'd guess about fifteen days up and a few more back, that is if we don't have Indian trouble. The horses will move purdy fast going up, but with the cattle it'll be slower. Blake, since we are leaving right away, I'm goin' to ride into town and pick up a few things."

Blake smiled at Gus, "And maybe see a little blond while you're there?"

"Could be," said Gus as he swung into the saddle on Pepper.

In town that night, Gus sat across from Annie at dinner.

"I don't like it at all, Gus, I'm afraid they plan to gang up on you when you get out of town!

"Annie, they don't know who I am. They think I'm just another hand. Besides, Sheriff Lacey will know about it, so I don't think they will try anything."

"Will you be staying here tonight?"

"No, I'll have to go back in a little while. I need to go by Johnson's store and get a couple of shirts, I don't want them to see the shirts I normally wear. They might see the badge holes in them and put two and two together like Charlie Wong did."

"Good idea," said Annie. "Come back by here before you go back to the ranch."

"I will."

After getting his shirts and supplies, he returned to the boarding house and went to Annie's room, "Come in," was the answer to Gus' knock at the door.

He took Annie in his arms, kissed her, and quickly turned to leave.

"That's it? That's all I get when you'll be gone for who knows how long?"

"I really have to go, Annie. You know what might happen if I don't."

"And you know I won't let that happen."

He paused, looked down at her, and seeing a tear on her cheek, he whisked her up in his arms, and kissed her long and hard; then he left.

His ride to the ranch was a lonely one. His thoughts of Annie and how he had to leave stung his heart and he heard himself say, "I'm not sure this job is worth it, Pepper." Pepper's ears indicated acknowledgement. "I guess you're thinkin' the same thing; it's a long way to Oklahoma, but you won't have to carry me all the time. There'll be other horses to share the load."

An extra day and they were ready to pull out.

"Blake, did Nobel put extra hobbles in the wagon? We'll need 'em."

"Yes he did. I'm purdy sure we have everything. The men left with the horses a while ago, and Noble left with the chuck wagon early this mornin'."

"Then I guess we had better move out. We need to get ahead of everybody and look for a place to bed down tonight. We will move up to the new Goodnight-Loving trail and take it to where it crosses with the Western trail at the Brazos, above Fort Griffin, and then go on up to Oklahoma on the Western trail. Rice said the place we are goin' to is east of the Friendship Store on the North Fork of the Red River.

They had no trouble on the way and when they arrived at the ranch of Hyrum Bodkin, he had seen the dust cloud of the horses and rode out to meet them. "I bet all you fellers are mighty tired. Bring the horses up to the house and put them in the pens there. There's feed for them and my man will take care of that. You can wash up and take a shower at the well-house and then come on in the kitchen . . . I think the cook has some steaks, and you're welcome.

"We can't thank you enough," said Blake Conway, "This here's Commodore Kelley. We call him Gus. He's ram-roddin' this bunch for Mister Stanford."

"Glad to have you fellers here. I want to give you Mister Stanford's bill-of-sale 'fore I forget it. You'll find, if you count, that there are more than is on the bill, 'cause it's been a good spring, and you'll have a lot of calves to keep up with. By the way, there are pens for your horses in the valley behind the house, and there's room in the bunk house for all your hands and there's beddin', too. That way you can get an early start in the morning."

Gus was set back a bit; he didn't expect to have a bill-of-sale for the cattle. *This sure is not what I expected. This is a lot of work and no payoff for me.* He examined the bill-of-sale before handing it over to Blake. "You take care of this for Rice, Blake, and I'll get the men ready to move out first thing in the mornin'. We've still got daylight, so we can get the horses put in the pens, and everybody can get a meal and a good night's sleep." There was nothing for Gus to do but move on since all was legal.

"Farley, tell Nobel to get a head start in the mornin', and that we'll be followin' soon. If he needs more supplies I'm told he can get them at Friendship Store as we go back by there. We need to get back across the river before a storm might blow in."

"Will do, Gus. How much of a lead should we give Nobel in the mornin'?"

"You know, Farley, with as much daylight as is left, I think it would be good if he went on to Friendship Store now and just bed down there. That away he'll *have* a good start, and we can get an early start in the morning. Tell him he can get a good meal here before he leaves."

Farley turned and headed to the wagon, "Nobel, Gus said to get a good meal and head toward that Friendship Store and get what you need there. That way you can take it easy and find a good place to bed down the herd tomorrow night. We can start early in the morning, Take Jeff with you to make sure you get back across the river.

"Dang, Farley, thank ole Gus for me. I won't have to hump it so hard to stay ahead of you fellers. What about the sugans? Won't they need 'em tonight?"

"Nope. The man says the bunk house is ready with all we need. I'll see you and Jeff at supper."

By the end of the next day the men reached the place Nobel had chosen to bed down the cattle and he had food already cooking by the time they settled the stock.

Blake and Gus dropped their saddles by a fire away from the cook fire. Blake looked at the cooking layout and asked, "Hey, Nobel. What's in the covered pot tonight?"

Nobel placed his fire hook on top of the pot lid and said, "It's a surprise . . . I picked them up at the Friendship Store."

"You picked what up?"

"Heck, Blake it won't be no surprise if I tell you. It'll be ready by the time the rest get here and get washed up."

When all were ready to eat with plates in hand, Nobel unveiled the surprise, "Here you go men: butter beans and cornbread!"

Blake had stood up to see what Nobel had, "Man alive, Nobel. You done real good. Them's my favorite! I'd never thought you could get them anywhere out here . . . load my plate!"

That evening some stood watch, and some had gone to bed, Blake, and Gus sat around the fire drinking a last cup of coffee, Gus commented, "These men have made good trail hands. They are purty good all around hands."

"Yeah, they've been good at Rice's ranch, and most have been there a while. Rice is good about giving a man a second chance. You plan to stay on a while, too."

"Not sure, Blake, I haven't figgered out what Rice wants with me yet."

Blake took a mouthful of coffee, looked at Gus and said, "What'a you mean, I guess he just felt like he needed another good hand, and if he asks me I'll tell him he's got one."

"Well I thank you for that, Blake."

Each tossed out the grounds from their cups and headed for their beds.

Chapter Eight

When the cattle were all penned on the north pasture at Rice's RS ranch, Blake and Gus washed up and went in to the headquarters to report to Rice about the drive.

Rice rose from his massive leather chair. "Well, I'll be doggone; I didn't expect you fellers back this quick!"

"We had good trail heardin' cowhands," praised Gus.

"The boys did exceptionally well," agreed Blake.

"It was like they had been doing it all their lives," added Gus.

"They had a good teacher. Gus treated them like they knew what they were goin' to be asked to do. It was a good ride. By the way, here's the bill-of-sale for the cattle."

"I can't thank you boys enough, and Gus, I thank you for taking on this task."

"Nothin' to it, Rice. They are good men. If you don't mind, I think I'll ride into town and stay there tonight."

"Sure, A bit anxious to see your lady friend, I guess."

"Yes, sir. It's been a while . . . she may have forgotten me by now."

"Oh, I doubt that. You go and relax for a while. I'll see you when you get back. You too, Blake, take a little time."

"Thanks, Boss, I'll be back soon."

"I'll look at the cattle while you're gone . . . I may want to change their brand!"

Gus and Blake rode into town together. Blake headed to the Gentlemen's Retreat and Gus toward the boarding house. He watched Blake, and once he went into the saloon, Gus turned up between two buildings and rode up the alley to Sheriff Lacey's house.

A gentle knock brought the Sherriff to the door, "Gus, where have you been?"

"We've been trailing cattle."

"Well, I was getting ready to go out there to Rice's tomorrow and give him what for."

"Why is that, Bob?"

"We've had another rash of rustlin' on both Hawk and Roscoe's place, quite a few head gone, and they're all fired up!"

"Bob, it wasn't any of Rice's men."

" What makes you say that Gus?"

"Cause all of Rice's men have been with me, all the way to Oklahoma and back!"

"Well I'll be doggone! Who'd you suppose . . ."

"I don't know, Bob, but I'll just bet that whoever it was didn't know Rice's men were gone. That sure puts a different light on this whole business."

"Bob, I may have to come clean with Rice, 'cause I'm goin' to have to investigate. After all, that's why I'm here: to investigate rustlin'."

"I'll let you do the tellin', Gus, but I'll be backin' you."

"Thanks, Bob."

Gus left the Sheriff's house and proceeded up the ally to the boarding house. Annie saw him as he stood in the doorway of the dining hall and immediately met him there. They walked into the hallway, and when they were out of sight, she threw her arms around him and asked, "Where have you been so long? I thought something had happened to you!"

Before he could answer she kissed him, then kissed him again.

"I made a trail ride to Oklahoma for Rice."

"Did you come to any conclusions?" she asked.

"Yes, I did."

"If they're not good don't tell me!" she looked into his eyes. "Oh, tell me anyway."

"You gotta give me a chance, Annie."

"Okay, I won't say anything else."

"I found out that Rice's men have not been doing the rustlin'."

"Who, then?"

"I don't know yet, but I plan to find out."

"So, you're going to be gone some more, I guess."

"Only for a little while."

"That's what you said before."

He took his finger and placed it beneath her chin, lifted her face so that her eyes met his, and kissed her long and firm, "I promise not to be gone as long as before. I'll make it a point to come back often."

"All right, but be careful"

Gus, faced with a hard decision, mounted his horse and once again headed toward Rice Stanford's ranch. Upon his arrival, Rice stepped out onto his porch and approached the hitching rack. "Gus, what are you doing back here? I thought you were burning to see that little gal of yours."

"I was, Rice, but a more important situation has come up. Can we go inside?"

"Sure, come on in."

"Are we private here, Rice?"

"Sure, no one else is home, LaRice has gone riding, Blake went with you, and the rest are moving the stock you brought back from Oklahoma . . . what is it Gus, you sound serious?"

"It is, Rice, and this is just between us right now."

"Okay, Gus, I'm listening."

"I haven't been square with you from the beginnin'. Because most townsfolk were sure it was you and your hands doin' the rustlin', I came to your place to see if I could gather any information. Actually my job is United States Marshall," Rice's expression changed to astonishment, "sent here because of the rustling. On our return, I found that the rustling was still taking place, and I knew it wasn't you or your hands, because they were with me, and I knew you couldn't do it by yourself."

"Gus I've been trying to tell those people all along it wasn't me! Just because some of my hands have been outside the law before, everybody just figured it was us!"

"I wanted you to know, 'cause now I will need to see if I can track whoever it was that took cattle from Hawk and Roscoe and probably from you, too."

Rice chewed the inside of his cheek, "I've got so many I probably wouldn't know if a few were missing."

"I plan to keep you informed. Sheriff Lacey knows it wasn't you, but won't say anything while I see if I can find out who is doin' it."

"Gus, if you need any help just ask for any of the men here you feel you can trust."

Rice, that's why I came to you, I feel I can trust all of your men."

"Thank you for that, Gus." And then tongue in cheek, he added, "I guess this means you're no longer one of my hands"

"I'm sorry I ran you a little short of help." Gus smiled and rose. "I'm goin' to start on your upper southwest corner and see what I can pick up."

They stepped out onto the porch and as Gus mounted up, Rice said, "Gus I appreciate your confiding in me, whatever you need let me know."

Gus rode to the corner of the RS ranch opposite from where Rice's men had taken the cattle to try to start tracking.

Pepper's ears flashed back as he said, "Well, Pepper, looks like we are lookin' for a needle in a haystack."

A snort from Pepper was the only response.

Gus spent the next three days tracking trails from each ranch to where the cattle were driven into the wide stream of Pot creek. Cattle had been taken from Rice's too.

"Pepper, now we know what all the cattle from each ranch had in common. They all wound up here at the creek!"

Having been out for three days, Gus' supplies were almost exhausted. "Pepper, I guess we'll have to pick up here later, we're goin' to have to get more supplies before we continue."

Gus rode to Rice's ranch, and Rice was more than happy to restock his supplies, "Anything, Gus, to clear my name with the townsfolk. Take what you will need. You're sure you don't need some backup?"

"No thanks, Rice. I've got a little more checkin' to do then I might need a few men to help."

"You just holler when you need us!"

"I will, and thanks for savin' me a trip to town. By the way, some of your cattle were stolen, too."

When Gus reached the creek again, he stepped down and walked each way trying to determine which direction they were taken. He mounted up and decided to go up stream first, then downstream.

He spotted tracks coming out of the water in both directions. "Now, isn't that clever, Pepper! They drove cattle both ways. Thing is, they didn't expect anyone lookin' for them to ride a couple of miles to find where they moved them out of this creek and drove 'em away."

He started to follow the tracks. The rustlers obviously didn't think anyone would follow from the creek, because they didn't bother to cover their tracks from the time they left the water.

Gus easily traveled about twelve miles following the tracks before he stopped and loosened his cinch to give Pepper a rest. He pulled a stick of jerky from his saddle bags and sat on large rock. "Pepper, these fellers were lucky; not much cover for a few miles to hide cattle, but I guess there's nobody to see 'em anyway."

The short breather refreshed him and his horse. He mounted up and continued to follow the tracks. After a few miles he entered fairly heavy tree growth, and he slowed his advance so as to not run up on anyone unexpectedly.

Soon his advance brought him to a clearing at the edge of the hill where he could look down into the valley below. He removed his glasses from his saddle bags and walked to the edge of the clearing.

"All right. Looks like we're in business. There are pens full of cattle." He spent some time adjusting the focus on several positions below and mumbled, "and if I'm not mistaken, and I don't think I am, I see at least two of Earl Roscoe's men in the bunch."

"Pepper, I guess we had better move from here 'cause it looks like they are getting ready to come back this way."

He led Pepper behind a pile of large boulders and waited for the four men to ride by. When they were out of sight he rode down to the pens to have a look at the cattle brands.

"Well now, I see they played no favorites . . . there are brands from all the ranches in this area.

Satisfied that he had found the rustlers, now he had to find and gather evidence on those he thought were responsible.

As he started to leave the pens, a voice boomed out from behind him above the braying of the cattle. "I don't know you. You got no business here . . . just loosen your gun belt and let it drop."

Gus dropped his guns and turned toward the voice.

As Gus turned, the man's face lit up in surprise, "Hey, I know you. You came to the ranch a while back, and you been workin' for ole Rice Stanford. Commodore. That's right. That's who the boss said you were."

Gus tried to place the man. "Just which ranch was that?"

"It don't matter. I work on both, and I got orders to shoot anybody that comes here,"

"Now how do you know that the boss didn't send me out here? You might just be in a heap of trouble if he did. Now, what'd you say your name was?"

"Jake. Well, the boys would'a told me, 'cause they was here a while ago."

Gus started to move toward the man. "The boss thought there might be some hoof and mouth disease in that last bunch of cattle, and he sent me out here to check on them."

The man lowered his gun and looked at the cattle, "You some kind'a vet or somethin'?"

"Something like that", said Gus as he moved closer to the man.

"I reckon that's possible, but I ain't seen no sick cows in this bunch,"

As he turned his head toward the cattle again, Gus reached out and snatched the man's gun from his hand, and with a quick right to the jaw, the man dropped like a sack of feed. Gus then dragged him toward a close shed. He was thinking as he dragged the man, *That's strange . . . he works for both Hawk and Roscoe. I wonder if they all work for both. He* slipped a bolt in the hasp, so that when the man revived he would have trouble getting out.

He buckled his guns on as he walked to Pepper and mounted up to ride toward Earl Roscoe's ranch.

Gus rode quickly to a position as close to Roscoe's ranch as he could and watched what was going on with his field glasses. It was getting late, but he was still able to see through the glasses.

"Well, I'll be doggone; Roscoe and the rustlers are sitting together on his back porch! I knew I had seen them when I was here before. Now, I've got to tie Roscoe into it all . . . and that won't be easy," he muttered to himself.

Gus moved to a shady area and decided to wait to see if these men might also work on the Hawk ranch.

He didn't have to wait long; all the men mounted up and rode toward the Hawk ranch. He followed a while, until he was sure where they were headed, and then he rode into town to Sheriff Lacy's office.

He rode up the ally to the back door, checked to see if anyone was in the area, and entered.

"Bob, I have some news that you're not goin' to believe."

"Sit down and tell me this news, Gus."

"I've located the stolen cattle and the ones that stole them."

"Don't keep me guessin', Gus, who is it?"

"A bunch of hands that are working on both the Roscoe and the Hawk ranches!"

"Are you sure? Earl and Jerald are the ranchers that wanted you to come and find out who was doin' it."

"Exactly! They both are. What better way to throw suspicion away from oneself than that?"

"I see. You 'spose it's them, or just their hands?" mused Sheriff Lacey, "Or did they get together and worked this out between 'em?"

"I figger they got together and worked it out so's they could blame Rice's bunch, and with the little action you were getting from Marshall Claxton they thought no one would ever catch on. Now I'm goin' to need Claxton to help get the goods on Roscoe and Hawk."

"I'll help too, Gus."

"I know you will, Bob, but I want you here to keep an eye out for four of their men. They got some extra money today, and I'll bet they will be in town tonight. If you have someone who can hang around the saloon, I'd bet they get drunk enough to loosen their tongues and spout off about their accomplishments."

"I have a man who can do just that."

"I'm not sure they'll talk in front of the saloon bunch what with them all lined up with Rice Stanford; but If we can get some evidence that they are behind this that's all we need. I'll check with you later, but right now I need to see if I can find Wade Claxton. He may not want to help since his term is up."

Gus left the Sheriff's office by the back door and walked down the alley. *Harve ought to know where Wade hangs out this time of day, he thought.*

When he got to the boarding house, he entered by the kitchen door.

As Gus entered, Harve turned to see who it was. "Hello, Gus, what brings you here?"

"Howdy, Harve. I was wonderin' if you might know where Marshall Claxton could be."

"Not for sure where he is, but he stays with the Barnes family when he's in town."

"Where is that?"

"It's about half a mile south of town. Just turn left on their road after you cross the bridge."

"Thanks, Harve, I'll head out that way and see if I can catch him."

Chapter Nine

Gus rode south toward the bridge. "Boy, Pepper, I'm gonna be in for it with Annie. I should have made it a point to see her while I was in the boardin' house."

It didn't take long for Gus to reach the Barnes home. He dropped his reins and knocked on the door. A lady answered the door. "Good evening Mrs. Barnes, I'm looking for Marshall Claxton. I was wonderin' if he might be here. I'm Commodore Kelley."

"Why, yes, the Marshall is in his room. Come in, and I'll call him."

Marshall Claxton came from his room pushing his shirt tail into his pants, "Kelley was it? Sorry, I was relaxin'."

"That's all right; can we step outside for a minute?"

"Sure we can. What's this all about?"

"I guess you know that your appointment is over. That's one thing I wanted to talk to you about. The other thing is that I've been appointed to take your place in this district. I don't know what they want you to do now, but I'm sure you will contacted. You know, of course, about the rustlin' that been goin on here."

"Yes. I've purtty much let Sheriff Lacey take care of that. It looks like Rice Stanford will take the fall for it."

"That's why I've come to ask for your help. Rice's bunch has had nothin' to do with it; his men are in the clear. I have determined who's behind it and where they've put the cattle. You don't have to do this you know."

"I know I don't, but this all sounds interestin'. It sounds like you've taken care of it . . . why do you need my help?"

"I don't have quite enough evidence on Roscoe and Hawk."

"Roscoe and Hawk? What makes you think they are behind it?"

"I trailed the men responsible. They were Roscoe and Hawk's men. I had seen them workin' on the ranches before. When they finished workin' the cattle, they went directly to each ranch, and I watched 'em get paid. The problem is, I have no proof that the payoff I saw was for the cattle."

"What can I do?"

"The Sheriff will have a man listenin' at the saloon; I need you to watch the stolen cattle while I approach Roscoe and Hawk directly. That will give us another set of eyes on the rustlers. You don't have to do anything . . . just watch. That way you will be safe."

"Fine. Just let me know where this pasture is. I'll get supplies and spend a few days observing."

After drawing Wade a map, Gus said, "You'll find a yahoo locked in the shed by the pens . . . you might better let him out and arrest him. If you have a problem there, I'll meet you on the hill above Roscoe's Ranch, 'cause I might need you to help arrest them." Gus mounted and headed back to the boarding house. Claxton gathered supplies and left to go to watch the stolen cattle.

When Gus arrived he looked for, but could not find, Annie. So he went to the kitchen.

"Harve, where is Annie?"

Harve turned, and then lowered his head, "I'm sorry, Gus, I forgot to tell you when you were here before. Annie's sister died in San Antonio, and she left to go to attend the funeral two days ago."

"When will she be back?"

"She didn't say."

"Did she leave a note?"

"No, sir, I don't think so; she was purty upset."

"Well, if she returns before I get back, tell her I'll be back in a few days"

"Will do."

Gus started to leave, turned and said, "By the way, Harve. You won't have to report to Rice about me anymore . . . he knows who I am."

Gus left and Harve stood and watched him go, then said, "Dang, I forgot to ask who he was. Now I still don't know!"

Gus eased Pepper onto the road that led to both the Roscoe and the Hawk ranches. What he didn't know was that Jake, the man Gus locked in the shed, had been able to get out of the shed and had ridden directly to the Roscoe Ranch.

Gus wanted to have a friendly conversation with Earl Roscoe to get the feel as to whether Earl might know what had been going on.

Earl did know, thanks to Jake's warning, so when he saw Gus coming, he posted his men to be ready when he called to them.

Because of his years of service, Gus tried to always stay alert of his surroundings. As he rode in, he glanced around, but saw nothing. Even so his nerves were on edge. He stepped down, went to the door and knocked.

Roscoe opened the door and said, "Well, Commodore. What brings you out here at this time of day?"

"Earl, I think we had better talk about the cattle rustling."

"I kind'a thought that might be why you're here." Came Earl's cool reply. He snapped his fingers, and two men walked into the room. Jake was one of them.

Gus smiled and said, "Hello, Jake; it's not so good to see you."

"I ought'a knock your head off," replied Jake.

Earl cut his eyes toward Jake. "Later, Jake."

Gus just kept smiling. "Don't be too hard on him Earl. I did hit him pretty hard, and left him locked in a hot shed. By the way, Jake, I sent a man to let you out."

"I'm still gonna let you have it . . ."

"I said let it go, Jake," snapped Earl.

Jake backed away. "Yes, sir."

"Get his gun and tie his hands, John, then take Commodore here out to the sweat box. You stay here Jake. I want him to be alive to enjoy his accommodations while I decide what we are going to do with him!" he said sarcastically.

Gus shook his head and said, "Maybe I should tell you, Earl, I'm not the only one who knows about this. And by the way, there are some pretty severe penalties for messing with a federal agent. What do you think your friend President Hayes will do when he finds out?"

"I don't plan for him to find out." Earl gave a chuckle. "I've known several people that have slipped into a draw because they went to sleep on their horse."

"And you think you can pull that off again?"

"It's likely I can. I saw you riding out here dozin' and bobbin' like you needed sleep. We tried to stop your horse before he went into that canyon, but I reckon he was dozin' too, ain't that right Jake?"

"Yes, sir, that's just how it happened, and it banged him up somthin' awful." Jake responded with a snear.

"Take him out there, John. We'll decide how to handle this later."

As John poked Gus with his gun, Gus said, "Guess I walked into it this time."

Jake watched John take Gus out and snapped, "I reckon you shore did. Some federal agent!"

Marshall Wade Claxton, found no one at the place where the rustlers had secreted the cattle. The shed where Gus had locked up the man was open, so he rode toward the hill above Roscoe's place where he had agreed to meet up with Gus.

John walked behind Gus as he was headed toward the sweatbox, so Gus didn't have much of a chance to do anything. He searched his mind for something that would help him get out of this situation, but nothing came to him.

The sweatbox was a small tin building about thirty feet behind the main ranch house. As they arrived at the building, John shoved Gus aside so he could get to the padlock.

Gus' hands were tied together in front of him. John's back was turned toward Gus, as he fumbled with the lock. So Gus made the most of the opportunity. He made a fist with both hands and swung at the base of John's neck. The force was great enough to stun him and he went down. Gus quickly took the knife from John's belt and cut the lashings that tied him. He also took his gun and stuck it in his belt and ran to the front of the ranch house where Pepper was still tied. He took the reins from the hitching post and swung into the saddle. He walked Pepper for a short distance to not make noise and then Pepper did the rest.

He checked back occasionally to see if he was being trailed, but saw no one. He rode on to the hill above the Roscoe Ranch where he agreed to meet Marshall Claxton. As he topped the hill, he saw Wade with his gun drawn.

"Not gonna shoot me are you Wade?"

"I couldn't tell it was you . . . where's your hat"

Gus stepped down and started to lead his horse toward a large rock formation, "It's a long story, but right now we had best take cover. Roscoe's bunch is probably not far behind. They were just about to do me in, but I managed to get away."

Wade led his horse behind Gus, "What'a you mean, *'Do you in'?"*

"The man I locked in the shed near the stolen cattle managed to get out. He was there when I walked in to talk to Roscoe. You can imagine the rest. I was headed to what they call the 'sweat box'. I could'a turned to toast in that thing! Only through carelessness on their part, was able to get away.

People like that sure make it hard to do our business, don't they?" said Gus running his fingers through his hair.

"We need to take Roscoe alive, and the other rancher, Hawk, too. Those two sent a letter to the President to get me here to see about all the rustlin' . . . tried to make everybody think it was Rice's bunch."

"They had me convinced. I just couldn't catch Rice's bunch doin' anything," said Wade.

Since John had not returned, Roscoe sent Jake to check on what was taking so long. He found John still unconscious in front of the 'sweat box'. Jake tried to revive him with no success, so he returned to report.

"Boss, John's laid out in front of the sweatbox, and I couldn't revive him, he's still alive."

"What about Kelley?"

"He's gone," Jake growled.

"I didn't hear no horse leave. Look out front and see if his is still there."

Jake went to the window, "His horse ain't here either!"

Roscoe turned and threw his drink into the fireplace. "Damn it, we've got to find him. I can't afford to go to prison . . . I've got too much invested in this place. Saddle the horses. I'll see if I can track which way he went."

Watching from the hill above the ranch, Wade alerted Gus. "They finally woke up, Gus. They're trying to find your tracks amongst all those other tracks out front of the ranch. Uh-oh, looks like maybe they found them. They're heading this way!" said

Wade as he slipped his rifle from its scabbard and balanced it on the rock in front of them.

Gus moved beside Wade. "We should'a gone into town and formed a posse, but that would have taken too long. What say we leave some good tracks for them to follow?"

Wade look questioningly at Gus. "Where do you want to lead 'em."

We'll head to Rice Stanford's place and give his men the opportunity to redeem themselves in the eyes of the people of Sykesville."

"Good idea," said Wade as they both mounted their horses.

They rode hard toward the Stanford Ranch, raising enough dust that anyone should be able to follow.

Riding side by side in order to raise as much dust as possible, Wade called out, "Do you think there will be enough men there to help make an arrest?"

"Rice has asked twice if there was a way to help, and I'd say this is it." Responded Gus loudly.

Gus gently nudged Pepper, and he was ready to go. They moved faster, hoping to be far enough ahead to get Rice's men ready to receive Roscoe's bunch. Wade and Gus rode into the Stanford courtyard in a flurry of dust. Rice's men had already started running when they hear the horses running.

The first man Gus saw was Rice's foreman, Blake Conway.

"Blake, Roscoe and his men are right behind us. I need you to help arrest them. Consider yourselves deputized."

Blake shouted Gus' instructions to his men, and told them to take a secure position and wait for them to ride all the way in.

"Thank you, Blake; I'm glad Rice told you who I was. We need to arrest Roscoe, so don't shoot him. We'll surround them if we can. Wade and I will leave our horses out front so they will come on in."

Gus ducked behind a wagon while the Marshall took cover near the side of the house.

When Roscoe and his men rode in, Blake Conway greeted them. "Well hello, Mister Roscoe. You fellers get down and rest awhile."

Roscoe responded, "We ain't got time. We're lookin' for Kelley. There's his horse. Where is he?"

Gus stepped from behind a wagon with his gun drawn. "Mister Conway asked you all to get down and rest, 'cause you are all under arrest!"

Stunned by the sudden turn of events, all of the men stepped down from their horses except Roscoe. As his men walked between him and Blake, Roscoe spurred his horse and was off.

"I need him alive!!" yelled Gus as he leaped on Pepper and was soon right on Roscoe's tail.

As Pepper overtook Roscoe, Gus reached across and knocked Roscoe off his horse. Gus was off his horse in a flash and jerked Roscoe up giving him an uppercut. Then he pulled the gun from his waste and held it on Roscoe. "Just stay down. I'll get to you in a minute," said Gus between gasps for breath.

Shortly, Wade rode up, "I was close enough to see all that, and I sure admire your skills, son, but I'm afraid I'm definitely too old to do that kind of work."

Gus had leaned against a tree and was still breathing hard. He grinned and said, "I'm kinda out of practice, too. I guess I should have shot him, but that would be too easy on him."

"Blake and the rest of Rice's men have taken the others into Sheriff Lacey's," said Wade.

"Good! He knows that Roscoe and Hawk's bunch are the rustlers. We can get a posse together when we get to town with Roscoe, and then go after Hawk and the rest of his men."

"Do you think we'll have a shoot out at the Hawk ranch?" asked Wade nervously..

"Not if Roscoe hasn't alerted him. I'll ride in first and see."

They took Roscoe in to town, and he was placed in a cell with the rest of his men.

"Well, Bob, we have half of the problem solved. We need to get a posse together to go to the Hawk ranch. I'll ride on ahead hoping he doesn't know about this action, but don't follow too far behind, 'cause he may get a little agitated when I tell him he's under arrest for rustlin'."

"I have twenty men standin' by, Gus, so we'll be there right away," said Sheriff Lacey.

"Thanks, Bob."

Gus mounted and patted Pepper on the neck, "Another ride and we can take a rest."

Pepper, a strong mustang, was ready and danced around before heading out.

As Gus turned, he faced toward the street and could see the boarding house. Annie flashed across his mind, but he knew he didn't have time to waste, so he rode briskly toward the Hawk ranch.

He continued to think about Annie, wondering if she had come back from San Antonio.

"You gotta keep your mind on business," he heard himself say aloud.

As he rode into the gate of the Hawk ranch he saw no one around. He slowly rode up to the front of the headquarters, stepped down and dropped the reins over the hitching rack and walked to the door.

He gave a knock and waited.

Soon the door opened, "Well, well. Lookie who's here, Mister Hawk. Gus Kelley. Come on in," said Hawk's man.

As Gus walked into the large living room accented with large ceiling beams, Jerald Hawk moved over to stand by the rock fireplace. "Sit down, Gus. Glade to see you. Have you made any progress on this rustling problem?"

Gus took a seat. "Yes, Mister Hawk. That's why I'm here."

"Oh? Well, that sounds fine."

"You'll not think so when I tell you what I found."

"Yeah? And just what *did* you find?" he asked while staring at Gus

"I found out what you and Roscoe have known all along."

"Well now, I don't know what to say."

"If I was you, I wouldn't say anything. Sheriff Lacey, Marshall Wade and a posse will be here soon to take you in."

Gus stood up. "It was a slick plan you and Earl had to put the blame on Rice Stanford and steal all those cattle. Unfortunately, Roscoe became a bit headstrong and struck while all of Rice's men were out of town with me!"

Hawk called, "George." When he did, a big man came from the other room with his gun drawn.

"I have to take you in alive, Hawk, 'cause the President will want to know how you played his friendship. But I don't feel obligated toward your men," Gus warned.

As Gus issued the warning, the explosion of a Colt filled the room. Gus felt the tug on his sleeve as the big man fired wildly as he was falling from Gus' shot.

Jerald Hawk looked down at the man on the floor, and all he could say was, "I'm impressed! If I had had a couple of men who could do that, you wouldn't be here."

As Gus was putting the irons on Hawk, Sheriff Lacey, Wade, and the posse rode up out front.

"Hawk, when we go outside, call off your men. We don't need any more killin' today."

When Sheriff Lacey arrived and saw how many men were there, he asked Gus, "With all these men and the ones from Roscoe's place, you gonna bust my budget!"

"*Uncle Sam* will take care of it, Bob. Just be sure none get away."

Bob looked at Gus and chuckled. "I forget you work for our rich uncle."

Marshall Claxton came in and looked around the well-furnished room at the Roscoe Ranch. "Boy, when both of these ranches shut down, and the railroad passes by, this town is going to fold like an accordion."

Sheriff Lacey chuckled, "I guess ole Rice Stanford'll get what he wants . . . 'the biggest ranch in these parts.' Well, Gus what are you going to do now that this is taken care of?"

"Bob, right now I'm goin' back to town to look for Miss Annie Shaw!"

Gus and Pepper hit the road to town at a pretty good pace. He patted Pepper on the neck and said, "Pepper, I promise this will be the last time I'll ask you to hurry for a while. We'll take a day off and just rest and eat, but I really need to get into town in a hurry.

Pepper never slowed. He kept a fast, steady pace until they were riding down the main street to the boarding house.

He tied Pepper to the hitch rail and loosened the cinch. "Don't let me forget to tighten that when I come back, or I'll be under your belly," he said patting the horse's neck.

He stepped up on the boarding house porch and went inside.

Behind the desk Helen Thomas looked up from her work and smiled. "Hello, Commodore. Haven't seen you in awhile."

"Hi, Helen. Is Annie here?"

"No she isn't. We haven't heard from her since she left."

A troubled look crossed Gus' face, "Did she leave an address where she would be in San Antonio?"

"Not that I know of. You might ask Harve."

"He already said she didn't leave one with him," he paused in thought. "There's probably over fifty thousand people there. Tryin' to find her is going to be hard. Thanks, Helen."

Gus went upstairs to pack a few things, and then he went to the kitchen.

"Havre, would you pack some good eats for the road. I'm goin' to find Annie. I'll need quite a few supplies. I'll bring a pack horse around in a while."

"That's good, Gus. We been worried about her being gone this long. Do you have any idea where she'll be?"

"Nope. But I gotta look. Did she say anything that might give me a clue?"

"All she said was that she hoped she got to see the Alamo again!"

After getting a pack horse, Gus loaded all the things he thought he would need and rode to the back of the boarding house kitchen door.

Harve helped him load the food.

"One more thing, Gus, I remembered she said her sister's name was Gloria Waddell. I hope that helps."

"It will, Harve. Even though she has died, that will help. I can maybe check the funerals done recently."

Gus slowly climbed into the saddle, patted Pepper on the neck and said, "Sorry Pepper, I promised we would rest and I intend to, but I want to ride out of town before I can get tangled up with somebody wantin' to talk. We'll get out east of here to the Pot Creek. If we need to, we'll spend a day or two. I've got oats and the grass is good . . . so we'll rest a bit. Before we go, I'm gonna borrow the sheriff's little black colt . . . just in case Annie will ride back with me."

He made arrangement with the Sheriff to use the colt, then he and Pepper headed out. They rode to the bend in Pot Creek where the grass was high and made camp. He took the load off the horses, hobbled the pack horse, and turned Pepper loose, because he knew Pepper would be stay nearby. "Now you have a little of this day and tomorrow. After that, I'll expect you to be ready to ride . . . It's a long way to San Antonio.

Gus flipped another small stick on the fire, finished the last of his coffee, and leaned back on his saddle to watch the sun slowly move to the horizon. "I just didn't realize how much we needed to rest." The cup slipped from his hand and he slept.

Chapter Ten

Nighttime had already engulfed the city of San Antonio. At the home of Annie's late sister, Gloria Waddell, Her brother-in-law, Jeff Waddell, moved across the room and lit another lamp.

Annie Shaw sat near the stove that had been lit to break the evening chill in the room. "Jeff, I really don't understand what you are asking; I need to get home and take care of my own business. I've stayed too long already . . . I should get back."

Jeff turned and walked back to where Annie sat, "Annie, I haven't told you the whole story . . . I've been offered a substantial business deal that is very important to me. I only got the offer because of Gloria. For years your father talked about her to Truman Allred. He offered to help, but since she has passed away . . . please, Annie. I'm afraid the deal might fall through if she is not here."

"Jeff, don't you think he will know that I'm not Gloria?"

"He never met Gloria in person, but he knew your mother when she was expecting you girls. Your dad just wrote to him about her, a lot, and probably sent a picture. I plan to ask him to meet me downtown instead of here at the house. That way you could casually walk in for a moment, and then excuse yourself after a brief reunion with him."

"What kind of a reunion could I possibly have when I know nothing about him?"

"He only knew your parents; surely you could carry on about something of your father."

"If I don't convince him that I'm Gloria it might cost you the whole thing!"

"I'm sure you can do it, Annie. I don't think you would have any trouble."

"Wouldn't it be better to just tell him Gloria passed?"

"No. He said in his letter he was looking forward to seeing her in person, and that is the reason he has agreed to come here."

"I don't know, Jeff. It doesn't sound right to me."

"It will be fine, Annie, I know you can do it. It will mean my company will be on a sound footing again."

"Again? I don't know, Jeff. I haven't gotten word back home yet about the extra time I've all ready spent here, and I know they will be wondering what has happened."

"You have good people taking care of your business for you. You said you didn't have to worry."

"I know what I said . . . but . . . there is . . . someone special. I don't know how he will take my being gone so long."

"Write him a letter, or send a telegram!"

"I don't really know where he is right now; he has so much going on."

"Well, you can send a telegram to the boarding house, and let them tell him."

Annie bit her lower lip, "I guess I could do that."

"Sure you can. Now, think about your father's friends . . . did he ever mention Mister Allred?"

"Not to me . . . that I can think of."

"Think hard, Annie, it's important!"

"I know it is, Jeff. I just don't remember anything about him."

Jeff paced a few steps near the stove, and then turned to Annie. I know . . . I'll go to the newspaper and look for information about Mister Allred. That might help. I'll look tomorrow; we still have a couple of days."

"I still feel uncomfortable, Jeff."

"Annie, listen. I've taken your money . . . I'll give it back as soon as I get this deal finished, then you'll be able to go home."

"What do you mean you've taken my money?"

"I was afraid you wouldn't help me, so I took your money last night, just hold on until I can find some information on Allred."

"I want you to know, Jeff . . . doing what you've done and what you're planning to do . . . I don't like it a bit."

"It'll be fine, Annie. I promise. You'll see."

Several days had passed since Jeff had taken Annie's money, and she was still waiting for him to find some sort of information on Truman Allred.

As Jeff readied to leave for his office, Annie approached him, "Jeff, I thought Mister Allred was supposed to be here already!"

"I got a telegram from him that he had been delayed and will be here tomorrow."

"Are you sure? I need to get home! You haven't given me money to send a telegram."

"He'll be here. Look, I found out that for a short while your father and Truman planned to open a business together here in San Antonio, but it fell through when so many people moved down here after the war."

"That was a long time ago, Jeff. Gloria and I weren't even born then."

"I know, but apparently they stayed in touch even after you were born, and since your older sister and you had left, Gloria was the only one that stayed home with your Dad. She is the only one he talked about to Mister Allred. So see, you won't have any trouble passing for Gloria."

"I still don't like it!"

"Look, tomorrow we'll ride into the office together and meet him. After a brief encounter, you can leave so he and I can talk. I'll walk you to the buggy and give you your money. He will be watching, so I'll kiss you on the cheek to convince him even more. Then you can leave.

After finally arriving in San Antonio, Gus found a livery stable and left his extra horses and packs, then rode to the Court House to find where he could ask about Gloria's funeral. He walked in, removed his hat and walked to the nearest cage and asked, "Sometime back a funeral was held for a Gloria Waddell, and I was wonderin' where I might find a funeral home that would know the Waddell residence?"

The clerk thought a minute, "You know I can give you that information . . . what is her husband's first name?

"That's just it . . . I don't know his name. I only know her maiden name was Shaw."

The clerk checked through recent death notices and then told Gus, "I have a Gloria Shaw Waddell, wife of a Jeff Waddell, but I don't know what funeral home conducted the service. There's a funeral home not too far away called Serenity Walk. If that's not the one, they can tell you where some others are."

Serenity Walk actually wasn't far away and it took only a few minutes to find it. When Gus arrived, he entered the large door with thick beveled glass. The door gave a slight moan as it closed behind him and it caused a chill to run up his back.

The man behind the large oak reception desk smiled at Gus as he removed his hat and asked if they had conducted the Gloria Waddell funeral.

The man looked up over his glasses, and, still smiling, said, "Waddell? That would be Jeff Waddell's wife. Young feller, I reckon you're in luck. Yes, we did his wife's service. Are you in need of similar services?"

"Me? Oh, no thank you!" Gus replied. "I just wondered if you might know where Mister Waddell lives."

"Yes, of course, you no doubt want to pay your condolences. He lives on Blum Street," he said as he took paper and wrote down the address, handed it to Gus. "Just go back up East Crockett to Alamo Plaza and turn right onto Blum Street. According to the number, it'll be about the third house on the right.

"I guess I am lucky, I never thought I'd find the information in all this mess o' folks, much less that it would be this easy. I sure do thank, sir."

"Well, you're quite welcome, son."

As Gus closed the big door behind him, the moan sent another shiver up his spine.

Gus mounted up and followed the man's directions. As he rode he thought, It's hard *to believe I could ride right into town and find them so easily!*

The house was a neat white bungalow set back away from the road. There were rose bushes and other flowers that looked well tended. A buggy with a driver was sitting out front. Gus sat on his horse and watched as a couple came out of the house to the buggy. Gus was sure it was Annie. She was dressed in a fancy dress, and she carried a small parasol to block the sun. They didn't see him, but he was pretty sure that the woman was Annie.

After the buggy left, Gus rode up to the house, dismounted and walked up to the window. *Well, this is the address and it sure looked like Annie getting into that buggy. Nice looking place. Nice furniture, a piano . . . he must do all right. I guess this is why she hasn't returned home.*

He turned to walk away when out of the corner of his eye he saw what he thought was a picture of Annie and the man on the desk. He turned back to the window, shaded his eyes to block the outside reflection to see if he was mistaken. "I don't understand . . . was there someone before me here in San Antonio . . . is that why she's been gone so long?" he muttered under his breath.

Gus mounted Pepper and quickly road to catch up with the buggy. They weren't in a big hurry and he caught up but stayed well behind to see where they were going.

The buggy pulled up in front of an office building and they got out and went inside. Gus dismounted and moved into the shade of a tree.

It wasn't long until Annie and the man came out of the building, he kissed her on the cheek, helped her into the buggy, and he went back inside.

Gus stood there stunned, *"So that's why she hasn't come home. I guess she found a better life than I could give her. Must be someone her sister and brother-in-law knew"*

Gus was heartbroken. He mounted, rode to the livery and picked up his horses and supplies and began the long, lonely ride back to Sykesville.

Chapter Eleven

What Gus didn't see taking place inside the office building he was watching, was that Truman Allred stood when he saw Annie and Jeff entering the room.

"Mister Truman Allred this is my wife, Gloria Waddell."

She winced when he said his wife and her sister's name, but she extended her hand. He took it and with a big smile, he said, "After all these years I finally meet you. I feel I've known you all this time, as your father told me so much about you as you grew up. He was mighty proud of you, you know."

"Yes, I know. I'm so glad to finally meet you. I won't stay long as I know that you and Jeff have so much to discuss. Thank you for helping Jeff so much."

"It's my pleasure, my dear. I am just so glad to finally meet you. You are every bit as beautiful as your father said. I have regretted not being able to go into partnership with your father . . . he was a fine man."

"Thank you very much, Mister Allred. Daddy was sad, too. Just so many came here after the war. I'm glad we were able to get together."

Annie moved to the door, and Jeff followed to help her into the buggy.

He said, "Thank you, Annie, I think he was impressed." He leaned over and kissed Annie on the cheek and turned and walked away. He didn't give her her money.

When Annie arrived at the Waddell house, she felt the emptiness of the house. She packed as many of her things as she thought she could take with her, placed the rest in the wardrobe, and changed into clothes for the return home.

Jeff had taken Truman Allred to the hotel and had gotten him settled, so it wasn't long until he returned to his home. He became very upset when he saw the clothes she was wearing, "Why did you change? You looked so nice in Gloria's dress," he asked.

"I told you, Jeff. I want to go home!" she declared bravely.

"Annie, I got the backing I need. You did great. Please consider staying . . . we could have a good life together."

"Jeff, I have my own life. I can't stay here and be Gloria; you must accept the fact that Gloria is gone!"

His pleading expression changed to anger, "I still have your money, Annie. Why won't you consider staying? I can give you everything you want."

"No, Jeff. You can't. You have nothing I want. I have my own life to live and you have yours. You need to get on with it!"

Jeff moved close to her, and reached out and took her by the arms, pulling her close to him.

"You would get used to it here; you would get to love me as I love you."

"You can't love me Jeff. You love Gloria, but I'm not Gloria, and you need to accept that!"

He reached out again, and pulled her closer trying to kiss her. She screamed and tried to pull away, "You're hurting me, Jeff!" She pushed herself away and hit him so hard that he fell back over a chair. His head hit a table on the way down and he didn't move. Annie froze for a moment. She was relieved he was still breathing, so she went through his coat pockets for his wallet. She removed the amount he had taken from her, and as he began to rally she grabbed her things and ran out the door.

When Gus returned from San Antonio, he went to the Sherriff's office.

"Gus! I'm glad you're back! A lot has happened since you been gone. By the way, did you find Annie?"

"That's a long story . . . I'll tell you later. But thank you for the loan of the colt. He wasn't ridden but he ate well. Now, what has been happening?"

"Well, sir, it took a long time to convict Roscoe and Hawk. They dodged a necktie party, but they was sent away for a mighty long time, and Rice Stanford has found favor with a lot of people in town . . . *town* . . . now that's something else. It don't look too good. All the shops and the boardin' house don't seem to be getting' enough business. And the railroad folks just won't listen to nobody; they won't come very close to Sykesville!"

"I was afraid of that. If the railroad won't come by, and the two biggest ranches shut down, I reckon the town will shut down too."

"Seein' as how I'm elected by the people, I may be out of a job, too."

"Bob, have you been out to either of the ranches lately?"

"Nope, but I hear they are deserted. All the hands that weren't arrested fled the country, or so I hear."

Gus rubbed his chin. "I'm wondering about somethin'."

"What's that, Gus?"

"I'll let you know later, Bob, I have some questions and I need to know some answers. I'll see you later."

At the livery stables, Paul Larkin met Gus as he entered. "You been gone a while, Gus and it looks like Pepper and the pack horse are kinda worn down to a nub."

"It was a long and rough trip, Paul. That's what I wanted to ask you about. I need to have a good horse and a pack horse; do you think you can help?"

"I shore can, that's my business. I gotta good, strong buckskin that can take you anywhere you want to go."

"Well, put my saddle on him and I'll be back. I've gotta get my pack ready too."

Paul looked at him and shook his head, "You beat all . . . how do you tell a body where you live?"

"I guess I live on the back of a horse, Paul."

"I reckon you do! I'll have the horses ready when you get back."

Gus rode to the county seat of Tom Green County to check with the land office. He asked his friend David Berkshire, the new Judge, to go with him.

Gus, David Berkshire, and the county clerk looked through the books on land claims for the homesteads and ranches in the county.

"We thank you very much, sir. It's just what I figgered. People outside the law will seldom think it important to use legal procedures for their property."

"You got that right! Every day I have people come in here crying because it wasn't done right," agreed the clerk.

He thanked David for his legal help, and when he had his business finished he rode back toward Sykesville. Since the Roscoe and Hawk ranches were in the general direction of where he was headed, and both headquarters were close together, he decided to check on Roscoe's place first and then Hawk's later.

"Well, Buck," he patted the buckskin on the neck. "I'll just bet there's a lot of hay in that barn."

He slipped the rod back that held the gate closed, and let it move of its own accord. The hinges gave a little squawk as it opened. He led the buckskin and the pack horse into the corral and stripped the pack and the saddle from them and rubbed them down. He pitched hay for them, and managed to find a bit of grain and put it in the manger. Then he proceeded to the main house.

As he entered, he noticed everything was neatly arranged as if no one had ever left. He moved into the kitchen and it, too, was neat and clean. Then he turned back toward the door when a scream pierced his ears.

"Hold on! I mean you no harm . . . who are you?"

"I am Rosita, I live here!" came the woman's terrified reply.

"Easy there, Rosita. I'm Commodore Kelley, the new owner. Why are you still here?"

"When Meester Roscoe was taken away, I had no place to go . . . so . . . I just stayed."

"They've been gone so long, how did you eat; how have you been getting along?"

"My cousin knows I am here; he brings me what he can."

"And you've been here since Mister Roscoe has been gone."

"Si"

"Well, I hope you have coffee and maybe a bite to eat. I've been traveling a good while."

"Sí, Señor. I have both. It will only take un memento."

Gus walked through the house, which had been kept as tidy as if Roscoe was still here.

"This place is beautiful, a man's dream fulfilled . . . yet all taken away because greed," he muttered to himself.

Gus, smelling the coffee, returned to the kitchen. "How long have you worked here, Rosita?"

"I have been with Meester Roscoe for twelve years."

"Twelve years? Incredible!"

"Si. The Mrs. was still living when I came."

"I must say, you have kept it looking wonderful."

"Gracias, Señor. I try."

"Rosita, I'll be spending the night, and I will see that you get the supplies you need very soon."

"Then I can stay, Señor?"

"Yes. How would the house stay in such good shape without you?"

She was still smiling as Gus went to the barn and saddled the buckskin.

He checked the Hawk ranch to see if it too was occupied and if any livestock needed tending. When he was satisfied that no one was there, he went back to Sykesville to Sheriff Lacy's office.

"Bob, I've found that the Orient railroads, which Gulf, Colorado and Santa Fe built in San Angelo, don't plan to come any closer to Sykesville for a long time, but they do come into Tom Green County."

With a troubled look Bob faced Gus. "I guess that means Sykesville will die on the vine like so many other towns that counted on the railroads," he lamented sadly.

"Could be . . . but maybe not."

"Do you really think we can stay alive?"

"Don't know for sure, but I think we can."

"How so?

"Well, just as I thought, Roscoe and Hawk never filed a claim on the land; they just moved in and settled."

"So? They lived there."

"But they didn't file on the land with the government."

"It would still be theirs since they built homes and lived there."

"Nope. They had to file to homestead it. The nice thing is I filed on both, and put them in my name."

"You what?" came a stunned reply.

"I filed, and they belong to me!"

"Gus, what about their kin?"

"That just it, Bob. They didn't own it, and they are not coming back. They had no family or kin, anyway."

"But still . . ."

"No buts about it. Legally it is now mine. There is no one on either ranch, well, on one there is."

"What do you mean?"

"A little Mexican lady called Rosita is on the Roscoe ranch. No one told her to leave. I told her to stay because she does such a good job taking care of the place. She cooks good, too."

"Gus, this seems so odd. It's like takin their homes from them."

"I know how it could look to outsiders who don't know the facts. But Bob, as a lawman you know they have a home now. They won't be coming back."

"I reckon that's right. To make the ranches pay, you'll have to have cattle."

"I know where they took all the cattle they rustled. You recall they rustled a lot of their own stock to throw suspicion on Rice . . . and the pastures on both places still have a lot of cattle. We'll have to separate Rice's cattle out and return them as well as anyone else's whose brands are in that bunch."

"I guess you have it all worked out."

"I've worked hard on it, so I hope so."

"What about the railroad?"

"We'll have to drive the cattle a ways after it comes into Tom Green County, but it's not like driving them to Kansas."

"True," replied the Sheriff.

As Gus started to leave, Bob said, "Gus, I know you have a lot on your mind about the ranches and all, but I think there's more. Something else is eating on you. It's Annie, isn't it?"

"It's Annie, all right. I guess I've lost her, Bob. I think she's found another life in San Antonio and somebody else to share it with."

"Dang, Gus. I'm shore sorry to hear that."

"Thank you, Bob. I'll see you later."

Chapter Twelve

Annie returned on the evening stage and went to the boarding house. She dropped her belongings when she entered, Helen screamed with delight, ran around the counter and threw her arms around her. "Annie, I've been so worried about you! I'm so glad you're back and all right."

"Thank you Helen. Has Gus been here today?"

"No, Annie, He went to look for you and hasn't been in here in a long time."

"He went to look . . . for me?"

"Yes. We were all so worried about you. Did you see him in San Antone?"

"San Antone? No. He probably couldn't locate my sister's place. Oh, Helen. I sure hope he will be in soon." She slowly gathered her things and went up to her room.

Days passed into weeks. Gus stayed on the ranch ridding over all the pastures, checking the condition and making sure there was water for the cattle. His days seemed to be a drudge since he couldn't get Annie off his mind.

Annie began to worry that Gus was still looking for her in San Antonio, so she went to the sheriff's office. When she entered, Bob stood and had a big grin on his face. "Miss Annie! Come right in. It's sure good to see you!"

She shook his hand, "Thanks, Sheriff."

"Gosh, Annie, don't you think it's about time you called me Bob."

"Thank you, Bob. Have you seen Gus?"

"Not in a couple of weeks. Haven't you seen him?

"No, I haven't seen him since before I went to San Antonio."

"Well, that's funny. He said he saw you in San Antonio, and thought you was gonna stay there . . . with another feller."

"He said he saw me in San Antonio?"

"That's what he said. He said he figured he had lost you. He's mighty shook up about it."

Annie was running all this through her mind when she finally said, "Oh, Bob, there's been a big mistake. Do you know where he is?"

"Well, he stays on the old Roscoe ranch when he isn't riding. He managed somehow to get both of those ranches."

"What do you mean he got both the ranches?" she asked puzzled.

"He can tell you that story better than I can, Miss Annie."

"Oh, Bob, may I borrow your little colt? I got to see Gus and clear up a *big* misunderstanding."

"Why, you shore can. I'll even saddle him for you."

'Oh, thank you, Bob. I'll be at your place as soon as I change clothes."

Bob put on his hat and headed to the back door, when he stopped, "Annie, he stays at the Roscoe house, and there's a lady there that takes care of the place named Rosita."

"Okay, Bob, I'll expect her to be there; maybe she'll know where I can find him."

Sheriff Lacy got the colt ready for Annie and it wasn't long before she hurriedly headed toward the Roscoe Ranch.

When Annie arrived at the ranch house, she grabbed the big brass knocker and rapped it a time or two and waited. Slowly the door opened and half a face peered out. "Si?"

"Rosita?"

"Si."

"I'm Annie Shaw, and I'm looking for Gus. Do you know where I can find him?"

"Come in, Mees Shaw. Meester Kelley has been out for many days in the pastures. I do not know which one. He has been so sad."

"I'll ride 'till I find him," said Annie.

Rosita watched as Annie stepped off the porch, "I think he has about used up his supplies, maybe he will be headed back."

"Okay, I'll watch for him."

Annie rode for hours until she saw what looked like a person a long way across a grassy field. She rode fast in that direction.

As she rode closer, she was sure it was Gus and she continued to ride fast.

Gus first saw the dust and then the horse. "What in the world? Someone riding like a bat-out-of-hell. Something must be wrong." He headed that way.

It wasn't long before Annie was close enough that he could tell it was her, so he stopped. Then he started to turn and ride away.

"Gus, wait!" she yelled. "Please."

Gus reined up and waited until she came up to him. He didn't smile or speak.

"Gus, Sheriff Lacy said you thought I had found someone else. I wanted to tell you that I have not!"

"Gus looked at her a long time, and then said, "I saw the picture of you and him."

"Picture? A thought hit her. You mean at the house? You were at the house?"

"I saw the two of you leave in the buggy, so I sorta looked through the window," he said, feeling a bit childish.

Gus, that wasn't me! That was my sister, Gloria."

I saw him kiss you," he mumbled. "Was that also your sister?"

"Gus, let me explain. Gloria and I are . . . were . . . twins! Gloria's husband was trying to get money for his business and it depended on the man that was a friend of daddy's meeting Gloria. I was there to meet him in her place. I didn't want to do it but he had taken my money and I couldn't leave, or even send a telegram. He promised my money back if I did that for him. The kiss on the cheek was just to convince the man more, because he was watching through the window."

Gus mulled that over in his mind awhile, and then a smile began to break on his face, "I don't know about the other guy, but you sure had me going. I've been dying all this time thinkin' you had found you a better life in San Antone."

"No, Gus, I couldn't come home, but I wanted to. I couldn't even send a telegram, because he had taken my money."

"Suppose we get out of this dirt and go to the house. If you're still in the mood to be with me, I got a surprise for you."

"Oh, Gus, yes. I've thought of nothing but you since you've . . . I've been . . . gone. Oh, dang it. You know what I mean!"

Gus stepped down, and pulled Annie off the colt, wrapped his arms around her and kissed her . . . then kissed her again. Then they both rode back to the ranch.

As they entered the ranch house; Gus tossed his hat at the hat rack and yelled, "Rosita, have you got any pie and coffee?"

"Si, señor, I have plenty," came her reply from the kitchen.

"Well, slice us a couple of pieces. We're hungry, and we have a lot to talk about."

Rosita came and filled their cups with steaming coffee. "Rosita, I guess you met Annie."

"Si," she said happily.

Well, you'll be seeing a lot of her from now on."

Once they finished their pie and coffee, they mounted and rode toward the Hawk Ranch. When they arrived, Annie stared at the beautiful adobe buildings surrounded by trees bowing in the gentle breeze drifting down from the hills behind. "Gus . . . I had no idea. This place is beautiful."

"In all this time you've not been here before?"

"No. I've never had the occasion to come here."

"Wait 'till you see the inside," he said wagging his eyebrows up and down.

They stepped up on the porch, lifted the latch of the large oak door and went inside.

Annie stood looking up and around in awe and said, "Gus, I would never have imagined how this place looks."

The ceiling was bolstered with large, heavy beams, the furnishings were leather and the floors were covered with beautiful Navajo rugs. They walked through the other rooms which were all equally elaborate.

"Oh, Gus, this place is beautiful!"

"It doesn't hold a candle to you"

"Oh, Gus, don't kid around now."

"I'm not kidding . . . It suits you."

"I just love it!"

'Well it so happens this entire ranch is now registered in my name, but it's yours. You'll have to live on it awhile. At least 'till we're married."

"That, I can do . . . did you say married? Oh, Gus that sounds so good."

"It's not going to be that easy; you'll have to hire a house keeper and hands to work your cattle."

"*My* cattle?"

"Yes, I told you there are cattle. There are some already in your pastures and the others . . . well, they just need to be moved to your pastures."

She was taken aback. Whoa! I'm not sure I can run a ranch."

"You can with help, and we'll get you some. Now, let's go back over to my place. I'm glad they built close together, I'd hate to be too far from you."

Gus noticed her face drop and asked, "What's the matter, Annie?"

She smiled quickly, "Nothing, Gus, I guess I'm just slightly overwhelmed." She had been thinking that living in two houses didn't sound as if they would be getting married.

They made the short ride to the Roscoe place. When they arrived, they stepped up on the big covered porch. Gus paused. "I'm gonna knock here because Rosita is still a little nervous about me just popping in."

He knocked on the big carved oak door. It slowly opened, but they couldn't see Rosita because she hid behind the door as it opened. "It's me, Rosita. Gus."

"Oh, you scared me, Meester Kelley."

"Rosita, Miss Annie Shaw; now owns the old Hawk place next door.'"

Rosita turned to Annie. "I'm very glad, Meese Shaw, that you will be so close."

"Thank you, Rosita. Me, too . . . I think"

Not only were the outside of the two ranches much alike, the interiors were much the same.

"Gus, these homes are incredible. I feel that I am intruding on someone else's home.'

"You are. This one's mine."

"Oh, Gus, you know what I mean."

"You'll get used to the idea when you realize that the previous owners are not coming back."

"But, what if they do? What about their families?"

"They are not coming back, and I checked. They had no families. It wouldn't make any difference. The ranches were not legally theirs . . . and you know me. Nothing but legal."

****

Gus had made a special trip with the buckboard to bring supplies and Annie's things from town to the house. As he brought them in, he said, "Rosita, again I want you know that you are welcome to stay on."

"Oh, thank you Señor."

"And Rosita, I just bet you have another primo or a hermana that might temporarily do as good a job as you to take care of Annie's place for a little while."

"Si, mi hermana, my sister, is called Miraposa. She can come right away."

"Good. So she is called butterfly."

"Si"

"Does that sound good to you, Annie?"

"That will be great," agreed Annie.

"Rosita, now that you have supplies, we will join you for supper. Once we deliver these things to Annie's house, we are going to take a tour of the out buildings and barns."

"Si, Señor, it will be ready."

"Annie I'm sure we can get help most anytime. Rosita's cousin has been taking care of her, and I would bet he can get us help to get the cattle back closer to the two ranches."

After exploring the barns and the other outbuildings, they went back inside the house and sat in the plush leather chairs.

" I can't help but wonder, knowing what kind of person Earl Roscoe was, if he purchased all this or stole it."

"It would have been hard to steal all this and get away with it, but he did sell a lot of stolen cattle."

"Maybe . . . but look what all he did get away with," she observed.

Gus stood up, caught Annie by the hand and said, "Well, that's purty much water under the bridge at this point. Come on. Let's see what Rosita has cooked up."

As they ate, Gus asked Rosita to sit down and eat with them.

"Oh no, Señor."

"Yes," said Annie, "by all means, sit down with us."

She hesitantly got her plate and sat down with them.

"Rosita, does your cousin know enough good men that would come to work here and the other place?"

"Si, Señor, we know many that would come to work."

"Good hard workin' honest men?"

"Oh, Si, Señor. Not like Mister Roscoe and Mister Hawk's men."

"Well, we have cattle to move, so tell your cousin to bring them around, and he can work here if he doesn't have a job already."

"Muchas gracias, Señor. He only works part of the time. He will be happy."

"We have to go back to town, but tell him we will start day after tomorrow. Does he have a horse?"

"Si."

"Good, tell him that we'll have to round up some more horses for the other hands, and the horses are a good ways from here."

"I will tell him."

"Thank you for the dinner, Rosita. I enjoyed it very much," said Annie.

As they got on their horses, Gus said, "I would like for us to go by Rice Stanford's place on the way back to town. Do you feel up to it? It's not too far out of the way, and I need to ask him to send some of his men with us to cut out his cattle from ours. Hey, that sounds good doesn't it? *Our cattle*."

"Yes it does, and I'm not a girl that has to be pampered all the time."

"I'm sorry. I want to be looking out for you."

'It's okay to look out for me, but don't worry about me. I'll let you know when I can't ride any more, besides I'll probably be riding when you've given up."

"Oh, you will, will you? Then how about I race you to the main gate?"

Before he could finish his sentence, Annie had gigged her horse and was kicking up dust in his face. He never caught her before she reached the gate.

When Gus got to the gate, Annie had turned toward him and was smiling, "What kept you?"

"That's not fair. You started too quick!"

"Oh, did I start early before you could start early?" she mocked.

"Okay, you caught me . . . I *was* plannin' to get a head start."

They started for Rice Stanford's place.

"Annie, just look out across this land . . . land that can make us a living, and we won't have to worry about whether the town lasts or not."

"But, Gus, what about the others that depend on the town?"

He thought about that and answered, "I guess you're right, Annie. Well, if we get permanent hands, we will need extra for them as well as supplies for the ranches."

"True, and extra people will keep the town alive, maybe. But I'm not sure about the boarding house," she sighed thoughtfully.

They were at Rice's ranch before they realized it.

They tied their horses to the hitching post and knocked on the door. While they were waiting, Gus asked, "Have you been here before?"

"No, I haven't," she answered.

"Well, stand by to be impressed. The places where we've been today can't hold a candle to this place."

The door opened. It was Rice himself. "Well, Gus Kelley and the lovely Miss Shaw."

"Hello, Rice, have you got a minute?" asked Gus.

"I sure have. You two come in, and I'll get you some refreshments . . . Befina," he called.

"Yes, Mister Stanford?"

"Maybe some lemonade, for our guests."

"Yes, Mister Stanford."

Annie spoke first. "Mister Stanford, you have a beautiful place here. I'm overwhelmed."

"Well, thank you, Miss Shaw, and call me Rice. Now what brings you by here today?"

Gus leaned slightly forward as if to speak confidentially. "Miss Shaw is now your nearest neighbor and I am her neighbor, and we just wanted to call on you to let you know."

With a questioning look on his face, Rice said, "I guess I don't exactly understand."

"Well, Rice, it's this way. Like most criminals Hawk and Roscoe had never legally filed on their places and since they hadn't, I have filed homestead rights to their land, mainly because they had no relatives and I want to keep it all legal."

"Well, I'll be dogged, I'd a never thought it, but sure wish I had," he said with a laugh,

"I hope you've filed on your land.

"Oh sure, long ago," said Rice.

"Good. I've come to let you know that when I get some hands to go get the stolen cattle, I will need you to send men to cut out your stock. Then we'll bring them home where they belong. I may need some help if we find other folks brands in there, too."

"Gus, you can count on us to help. You've helped me become an upstanding member of this community, as I have always wanted to be, and for that I can never thank you enough."

As Befina served them lemonade, Rice's daughter, LaRice, came into the room. "Hello, Mister Kelley and Miss Shaw."

Gus stood, "Hello, LaRice, nice to see you again."

Annie smiled and nodded in recognition.

"LaRice, Mister Kelley and Miss Shaw are going to be our neighbors."

"Really? Oh, that's nice; I'll have someone to visit when I go riding."

"Yes you will, anytime; however, we'll have to set up housekeeping first," said Annie.

"Oh, Miss Shaw, may I help? I've kind of been studying design, and looking at a lot of magazines about modern tastes."

Rice frowned a little and said, "LaRice, you must be asked, don't butt in."

"Oh, but I would be glad for her to help me, Mister Stanford. It needs a feminine touch, and I've been cooped up in that boarding house for so long, I have no ideas on home décor . . . not that I need much."

LeRice excitedly said, "Just let me know when, Miss Shaw!"

Annie stood beside Gus. "Mister . . . Rice. I enjoyed the lemonade, but I must get back to the boarding house. I've been away too long."

Rice stood. "I'm glad you stopped by, and I'm glad, too, that you two will be our neighbors. That way I won't have to worry about rustlers . . . will I?" he laughed.

"No sir, that's one thing we shouldn't have to worry about anymore. Good day to you then."

Gus turned to Rice, "I'll let you know when I get some hands to work the cattle."

"Fine, Gus, I'll be ready."

Chapter Thirteen

At dinner that night, Gus and Annie sat at the back table where it was not as bright as the rest of the dining room.

"Gus, I can't get over the changes in my life that you have brought since you have been here."

"Annie, it's no more than you deserve."

"But, what am I going to do with both a boarding house **and** a ranch house? I don't think I can handle both."

"You can let me help you. I'm sure that Rosita's sister is a good cook and house keeper. We'll manage; don't worry."

"Okay mister fixer upper, I'll rely on you!"

"Good, now let's eat, I'm wore out and I bet you are, too."

"I still have some work to do. As you know, I've been gone a long time."

"I'm well aware," Gus admitted.

When they had finished, Gus stood and said, "If you are going to continue to work, I'll see you in the morning."

In his new home, Gus was up early the next morning, since he was to meet the new hands at the ranch. As he washed his face at the wash stand in his room, he looked out the window just as the sun was coming up, he said aloud, "Boy, that's something to watch. You couldn't see that in Virginia . . . too many trees. I think I'm going to like it here."

Annie had asked him to breakfast this morning at her house. And when he had finished, he rode back home to meet the men Rosita's cousin had gathered.

The men were waiting in front of the main building. One man saw Gus approaching and moved forward to meet with him.

Gus stepped down, and when he did, a young boy ran forward and took Pepper's reins and led him to the hitching post.

"Buenos días, Señor Kelly, I am Emilio Estrada, Rosita's cousin," he said with a friendly smile.

"I see you were able to round up a few hands." He chuckled as he surveyed the gathering

"Si, they are all good, hard-working men and they are honest."

"That's certainly a glowin' recommendation. Did you tell them we wanted them to stay here on the ranch to work?"

"Si, I toll them."

"Good! We can probably use some more men since we will work this ranch and the Hawk place. We plan to give the ranches new names before long. But first we will need to move cattle from a place about twenty or more miles north of here back to these ranches. Hands from Rice Stanford's ranch will help us, because some of his cattle are there, too. Do all of these men have their own horses and rigs?"

"Si, they are ready. They have their bedrolls too. They have, as you say, the experience."

"Okay, then, tell them to put their bedrolls in the bunk house and let's get started. We don't have any supplies, so we will need to try to make it back before dark. Rice's bunch will meet us at Pot creek. From there we'll ride to the cattle."

There were so many cattle, it ended up taking two days just to separate them. Cattle from the Roscoe, Hawk and Stanford ranches, as well as two others, would have to be returned later.

Gus wiped sweat from his brow with his neckerchief as Rice rode up beside him. "Well, Rice, you've saved our bacon again."

"Oh, how's that?"

"I underestimated the number of cattle and how mixed up they were. I thought we could get through a lot quicker than this and didn't bring supplies. We sure were lucky you sent a chuck wagon with enough food and coffee to take care of us. I owe you."

Rice looked at Gus and grinned. "Shoot, you don't owe me anything . . . after all, you set me straight with the people around here; if anything is owed, it's from me."

"Maybe we'll just call it even, then. I guess we can leave the other ranches' cattle here until we take care of our own. I'll come back in a few days since they have feed and water."

Rice started to ride off when he stopped and turned to Gus. "I'll see you later, *neighbor.*"

Gus sat his horse and watched Rice ride off. A big smile slowly spread across his face.

While the men were penning the cattle behind the ranch house, Gus rode under the sign that declared the ranch to be that of Earl Roscoe. As he did, a rifle shot cracked and the bullet embedded in the lower part of the sign just above his head. Gus rolled off Pepper with his rifle pulled from the scabbard, and popped him on the rump so he would run out of the way. Then he crouched behind the trunk of the tree that formed the leg of the sign.

As he sat there wondering what had happened, another bullet ripped bark from in front of his face. "What the blazes is going on?" he muttered. "I can't tell where those shots are comin' from."

Since Gus had not returned fire, the shooter was not certain if Gus had been shot or not. Gus eased around behind the trees and brush that grew from the entrance all the way to the smokehouse.

He quickly spanned the distance between the smokehouse and the main building that had a little cover, and he eased to the window beside the back door. Looking in the window, he saw Rosita hovering in a corner crying.

He gently tapped on the window, and got Rosita's attention. She looked toward the front room of the house and then out the window to Gus. She looked back toward the front again and then moved across the room to let Gus in.

Gus whispered, "Who is it, Rosita?"

"It is Mister Roscoe!"

Gus was stunned. "Roscoe?" he whispered . . . How in the world?" his voice trailed off. "Is anyone with him?"

"No, Señor, I don't think so, I believe he is alone." she replied softly.

Gus slowly eased through the house to the front. When he reached the doorway to the living room, he leaned in cautiously to locate Roscoe. Then he stepped into the room. "Drop it Earl, it's over."

Earl Roscoe spun around so fast he lost his balance and sat back on the floor with a loud thump. He couldn't get his rifle swung around to get a shot, so he dropped it onto the floor.

"Just what are you doing here anyway?" demanded Gus.

"I've come to claim my ranch. I understand you are trying to steal it away from me."

I don't have to take it away from you. You never owned it. Besides, what are you doing out of jail?"

"Hawk and I know people in high places. We don't have to stay in jail. We've been pardoned."

"Pardoned? By who?" asked Gus.

"By the Territorial Governor of Oklahoma!"

Gus shook his head in amazement. "Well, this is not Oklahoma, and your relations with the President have been canceled. I don't know why you were taken to Oklahoma, anyway, but now you're goin' to Huntsville! Is Hawk at his place?"

"I don't know where he is. You got no right to lock us up again!"

Gus put the hand irons on him. "I have every right. With the crimes you two have committed, you should have been hanged instead of going to jail!

"Rosita, have your cousin come in and stay with you until we know that none of his men are comin' around."

"Si, I will tell him."

"I'm going to take this one to town."

Earl Roscoe stumbled forward as Gus pushed him toward the door. "You don't think I came alone do you? You won't make it far when you're out that door." Roscoe informed him.

"Well, Earl, if you've got a shooter out there, he's liable to shoot you since you're goin' out first."

As Gus pushed Earl out the door, Earl dropped to his knees. When he did, shots rang out. Bullets splintered the door jamb beside Gus' face. He stepped back behind the thick oak door and located the shooter. When he tried to returned fire, more shots came from the trees.

Earl was trying to get to his feet but he had trouble getting his balance with his hands behind his back. Gus quickly reached out and brought his 44-40 down hard on Earl's head and continued to return fire.

Splinters from the door frame had hit his face and blood was running into his eyes making it hard to spot the shooters. He yanked off his neckerchief and mopped the blood from his eyes. More bullets thudded into the heavy door. Each time, he watched where the smoke from their guns spewed out from behind the trees. When he was sure he had them located, he took Roscoe's rifle and made quick work of two of the shooters. The shooting stopped.

Gus shouted to Rosita, "All is clear, Rosita. I'm takin' Earl to Sheriff Lacy. Have Emilio take care of the men out front, please." He took Earl Roscoe by the collar and jerked him to his feet and put him on the horse he had ridden in on and led him to the gate where Pepper stood waiting.

After he took Earl Roscoe to the jail, Sheriff Lacy offered to go with Gus to the Hawk Place.

"Thanks, Bob. I can use the help." They rode at a fast pace and when they arrived at the courtyard gate, they were greeted with rifle shots.

Gus and Sheriff Lacey hurriedly moved behind the huge rocks that lined the side of the entrance, and each pulled their Winchesters from their saddle boots. Then they waited and watched to see where the shooters might be hidden.

"Can you tell how many there might be, Gus?"

"Nope. More than one, though! I think there are two in the wood shed and at least one in that wagon by the main house. I think I can get close to the wood shed if you'll keep 'em busy."

"I can do that; just be careful."

Bob began firing as Gus slowly moved behind the rocks and trees that were along the courtyard fence until he was even with the shed. He moved so he was at an angle to look right into the door. He waited until a man inside started to return the sheriff's fire When he did, Gus was able to get a shot that dropped one, and he rolled out the door. He waited for the next man to take a shot, and when he did, Gus shot him too.

By this time Sheriff Lacey had moved in the opposite direction, and he was drawing fire away from Gus as Gus began moving toward the main house.

Gus, running full speed, hit the side door which flew open with a loud bang. The noise of the door caused both men inside to stand up. Sheriff Lacy shot one as he became visible through the window. The other man was Gerald Hawk.

"Okay, Hawk, put your gun on the floor and move away from it"

"I got a right to defend my home!"

"You don't have a home; you forfeited all when you decided to go against the law."

"What'a you mean? This is *my* home!"

"I'm afraid you and Roscoe didn't do your home work. The law that you and he felt didn't apply to you has specific requirements you didn't bother to consider. Your release by Oklahoma authorities is null and void. You're joining Roscoe at Huntsville!"

"But . . ."

"No buts about it. Sheriff Lacey will take you now. Any more of your men around?"

"Just the four of us." He snarled.

"Then you're lucky you didn't join the others."

"You call going to Huntsville lucky?"

"Well, at least you are still goin'." Gus responded.

Chapter Fourteen

When the cattle were tended to and hands were hired for both ranches, things began to run smoothly. Gus began to ride both ranches checking each of the ranges where the cattle were placed.

As he rode to the northern-most range, he could see the line shack in the distance, "Pepper, if I'm not mistaken I see smoke from the Detrick line shack."

He rode closer and stepped down in a small grove of oak trees. He took his field glasses from his saddle bags and found a log where he could sit and watch the shack. *It's not cold enough for a fire, so they must be making coffee. I could sure go for some right now.*

After having watched for a while and seeing no activity, he decided to approach the shack. He approached on foot and stopped to listen near the door. He could hear voices but could not make out what was being said.

He decided to take the bull by the horns. He took the thong off his Colt, lifted the latch, and stepped inside. Two men sitting at a table in the middle of the room stood up as Gus entered. "Howdy, we've been wondering when someone would get here."

"Now, tell me what are you doing here anyway?"

The men looked at each other, and then one spoke up. "Why, we're waiting word from a Mister Roscoe. We are supposed to go to work on his ranch."

"Well, gentlemen, I'm afraid you're going to be disappointed. Roscoe doesn't have a ranch and is on his way to jail."

"His man told us he was wrongly accused and got out of jail!"

"Sorry, but that's not quite the way it is. Where are you men from?

"We come down from Oklahoma territory."

"You had best head back that way. There's nothing for you here."

"But we come here for a job and we come a long way!"

"I reckon you have at that. Say, you men on the right side of the law?"

"Yes, sir. We hadn't had **no** trouble with the law."

"That's right. Neither one of us!"

"Most of Roscoe's men are on the wrong side. I figgered that's why he hired you."

The two men stood looking bumfuzzled.

"No, sir. We never met Mister Roscoe. We was hanging around the livery stable when one of his men asked us if we wanted to work and drew a map of this place and told us to wait 'till we heard from him or Mister Roscoe. He said there was enough supplies here 'till he got here."

Gus rubbed his chin. "I see. All right, I can use a couple of good hands."

"We'll make good hands; you'll see," the men agreed readily.

Gus moved toward the door, "I'm goin' to check the water in the pond at the foot of the hill. Put this place in order, get your gear and some of the supplies, enough for a day or two, and meet me down there. We'll ride out some of these pastures. By the way, what are your names?"

The first man spoke up. "My name's Jess Simmons."

The second man said, "Slade Gibbons."

"You fellers can call me Gus," Then he walked out the door.

The three men rode the pastures for two days, until their supplies ran low. Gus eased Pepper down a small rise to a stream running beneath a heavy deposit of rocks. He stepped down and loosened the cinch, and let Pepper drink in the cool clear water. When his horse finished, Gus dipped his neckerchief in the water and bathed his neck, "With this many trees around, a man don't get a lot of breeze."

The other two agreed as they sat down beneath a large oak tree near the rocks.

Gus squatted down beside the stream to wet his neckerchief again when a rifle shot rang out. The bullet zinged off into space. Gus took his hat and flagged Pepper away, which took little effort as Pepper was on the move already. Gus dove for a place behind the rocks.

He scanned every foot of the horizon.

Without looking at them, he spoke to the two men who were now flat on their bellies under the ledge. "Maybe he only saw me, so you fellers stay out of sight; but keep an eye out. I'm going to see if I can get closer. There wasn't anybody else with you was there?"

Jess Simmons spoke up. "No sir. Not with us. Who you reckon would be takin' a shot at you?"

"Someone Roscoe or Hawk hired like you, I guess. Only he told them what he intended to do. This is probably the one coming to get you two.

"We have actually gone in kind of a circle and are not too far from the ranches. I cleaned out most of their men . . . must be at least one man who didn't get the message. Stay here and I'll see where he is."

Another shot rang out clipping a small limb from the tree over Gus' head. "I've got you now, hombre," he murmured as he opened fire with his rifle toward where the smoke spewed out from beneath the trees."

They waited a while. No more shots came. Not even when Gus stood to move ahead, so they thought they were in the clear.

The three of them, guns ready, began moving cautiously to higher ground. They searched together for a while but found no tracks of anyone else. When they decided to fan out in three different directions, a branch cracked a warning. Before Gus could turn he heard the shot and felt the impact. The shoulder wound sent him to his knees, but even as he went down, his Colt was answering the call and the man crumpled.

Gus stood over the man who was still conscious, but fading fast. He grabbed the front of the man's shirt and lifted him up. "Who sent you out here to shoot me?"

The man's eyes were rolling back in his head, "Answer, man, you don't have much time!" Gus shook him to bring him back to consciousness. "Who was it?"

The man's breath gurgled through the blood beginning to well up in his mouth. In a whisper he finally got out the word, "Hawk". Then he was gone. They took time to bury the man in a wash-out near the stream, and placed rocks to deter animals.

Since they were near the ranch, Gus decided to stop the bleeding and wait until they arrived to consider his wound.

Jess Simmons spoke up. "I sure hope we won't have to dodge bullets any more on this job! I might should'a gone back to Oklahoma."

"Hopefully this will take care of the problem. The head honchos are going to jail.

From that point on, Gus determined to watch more carefully before walking into a situation that might be questionable.

When they arrived at the Roscoe Ranch, Gus introduced them to Emilio Estrada. "Emilio is in charge. He'll show you where to store your gear and where to bunk. I'll see you at supper."

When he walked into the main house, Rosita was there to greet him. "Señor Kelley! Señorita Shaw asked that you come to the Hawk after your supper."

"Thank you, Rosita. Was Miraposa able to help out getting the other place in order?"

"Si, she did and we thank you so very much!"

"Sure. I'll ride over as soon as I finish eating. We've been out a long time with not a lot to eat."

"I can bring yours now."

"Good. Oh, we have two more men, a Jess Simmons and Slate Gibbons . . . who will be eating with the others. Emilio is taking care of them now."

Rosita started to go back to the kitchen when she noticed the blood on Gus' shirt, "Señor Kelley, you are bleeding! I will get things to take care of it."

"Thank you, Rosita, and please bring another shirt from my room."

Rosita cared for Gus' wound, left a fresh shirt, and then went about her work. He carefully put on the fresh shirt and went to the stable. Instead of Pepper, he asked for help putting his saddle on the Bay that he had ridden before. "Pepper, you take it easy for a while. Buck and I will take this ride while you rest," he said as he gave Pepper a pat on the rump.

Riding to the Hawk Ranch didn't take long, but the sun was drifting toward the western horizon.

Gus stepped down and loosened his cinch. He used the heavy brass knocker to announce his arrival.

Annie greeted Gus with open arms and a big kiss. "Where have you been so long? I was worried that you got caught in another ambush!"

Gus flinched a bit when her hand accidentally brushed his wound.

She noticed his expression and asked, "What is it, Gus? Are you hurt? What happened?"

"It's okay, Annie. We ran into another of Roscoe's men who didn't know he went back to jail."

"Are you all right?"

"I'm fine; don't worry about it Rosita dressed it for me."

"I can't help worrying about it . . . I don't want to lose you!"

"I plan to hang around for a long while," he said, pulling her close. "I was thinkin' as I rode in, It's about time we named these ranches something else. I'm tired of sayin', 'The Hawk' and 'The Roscoe'."

"We can call them the 'Annie' and the 'Gus,'" she said laughingly.

"I'm serious, Annie."

"I know you are, silly! I've been thinking about it, too. How about calling them 'The Commodore Ranch" and 'The Tree Top Ranch', since this place is higher than yours."

Gus didn't answer right away, "You know, that doesn't sound bad at all. "The Commodore' and the "Tree Top." Matter-o-fact, it sounds good! We'll have to come up with brands to suite the names."

Annie rolled her eyes, "Let's not do that now. We have better things to do."

"Such as?" asked Gus curiously.

"I have a fire going to knock off the chill, and I thought we might sit and . . . and talk a while."

"You know, I've been thinking *that* for three or four days now!" said Gus, as he smiled at Annie.

They moved to the divan in front of the fireplace and just stared into the fire a while saying nothing. Gus put his arm around Annie, and she laid her head on his shoulder.

Gus looked at Annie; she smiled, and he said, "It's nice here, isn't it?"

"It is . . . Gus, before you walked into my life that day, I couldn't have imagined anything like this ever happening to me."

"You can't imagine what happened to me that day. The picture of you standing there behind the counter, sun shinnin' on your hair, is one that will never leave my mind!"

"You seemed nervous that day."

"I was. You took my breath away."

They looked into each other's eyes a moment, and then kissed.

As they parted Gus cleared his throat and said, "It's getting' late, Annie, I'd best get started home."

"Do you really have to? Don't forget this house has many bedrooms, and Miraposa makes a mean omelet."

"It sounds tempting, but right now I'm not sure about myself." He looked at her and smiled awkwardly.

"How has Miraposa worked out?" he asked, to change the subject.

"She has been a great help getting the place in top order, but she says she will have to get back soon."

"Well, we will work out something when she has to leave. But right now I need to get ready for a long trip tomorrow."

"A long trip?" she asked frowning.

"Yes, when I reported what the Oklahoma judge did with Roscoe and Hawk, I was asked to go there and find out what's going on."

Exasperated, she replied, "Oh, Gus, It seems you are gone all the time!"

"I know, but it won't be for long. After this trip I plan to resign and become a rancher."

"How long will you be gone?"

"Not sure. Hopefully not too long."

"It seems like your 'not too longs' turn into 'long time gone'," she remarked dejectedly.

"This will give you time to get your ranch in order and get acquainted with your cowboys."

"Hummm . . . *get acquainted with my cowboys.* That sounds nice," she said smiling mischievously.

"Just don't get any ideas, now." He pulled her close and kissed her, "You wouldn't want any bloodshed around here."

"You mean you would fight over me?"

"You bet your boots I would! I better go. Now!"

Annie walked him to the door. He held her close, they kissed, and Gus said, "You don't know how hard it is to leave right now."

"I know how hard it is to watch you leave," she replied quietly.

"I'll get back as soon as I can. There's something I need to ask you."

"Don't leave me with a statement like that!"

"All right, Miss Annabelle Shaw. As soon as I get back, I want you to marry me . . . will you do that?"

"Yes, Mister Commodore Kelley! I will marry you! You know, I've been wondering just why you've fixed up two places. I was beginning to think we would always be apart."

Gus took her by her shoulders, pulled her close, and kissed her again. Then he gently pushed her back, looked into eyes that were filled with tears of happiness and said, "I'll rush back as soon as I can, and it won't be long 'till we move you into my ranch!" He turned and walked toward the door.

"What? And here I was thinking you would move over here," she said blinking her eyes innocently. They laughed as he walked out the door.

Chapter Fifteen

He left the next day riding Pepper and leading two pack horses.

The trip to Fort Sill, Oklahoma Territory, would take him a little less than a month if he had no trouble on the way.

By midsummer, he arrived and began his search for Judge Randle Straight.

The first place he looked was at Barnes and Freeburg law offices. Gus opened the door. As he entered he heard a small bell tinkled his arrival.

"Come right in . . . may I help you?" The sound of the voice came through a door at the back of the office. Soon a man dressed in a grey suit appeared.

"I hope so. I'm Federal Marshall Commodore Kelley, and I'm here in town lookin' for a Judge Randle Straight."

The man's eyebrows went up. "Oh. I'm sorry to say that Judge Straight was gunned down last week in the local saloon. Is there something else I could help you with, Marshall?"

"I guess not. How did a thing like that happen?"

"A local man wasn't too pleased with a judgment he handed down."

"That makes two of us, I guess," said Gus, running his fingers threw his hair. "But I didn't plan to shoot him."

"Oh? Had a little trouble with a judgment, did you?"

"You could say that . . . I came here to arrest him for a couple of decision he made."

"I see. Someone saved you some trouble. Is there anything else I could help you with?"

"Maybe so. Do you know where I might find a feller who might just be your competition, by the name of Gregory Baines?"

"Why, yes I do. He's no longer in practice. He just retired. You'll find him at the end of this main street in a little yellow house. His name is still hanging from his mail box."

"Much obliged to you for the information."

"Sure, Marshall. Come back any time."

Gus mounted up and led his pack horses to the judge's house. He tied Pepper and the other two horses to a tree limb, stepped up on the porch and knocked.

The door opened revealing an older man with grey hair holding a book in one hand and his glasses in the other. "Can I help you young man?" he asked, squinting at Gus.

"If you are Gregory Baines, you can."

"Well, then, come in and tell me about it." As he turned and walked back into the room, Gus followed.

"You come far? You look a little dusty." He motioned to a table nearby, "There's a little somethin' to take the dust out of your throat."

"No thank you, sir. I'm fine. I rode up from Sykesville, down in Texas."

"Ah. That's a long ride. Go ahead and sit down; you didn't say who you are."

Gus took a seat opposite the chair where Mister Baines sat. "I'm Federal Marshall Commodore

Kelley, and I came here to arrest Judge Randle Straight."

"Dang, you're just a little late. Somebody shot him last week."

"That's what I hear, and that's what brings me to you. Your government wants you to be the Federal Judge for this part of the territory . . . the area that was Judge Straight's. They sent me here to arrest him and swear you in as the new judge."

"Well, young fellow, what made them think I'd take the job, I just retired?"

"Well, sir, they have seen your record and they thought you would be the best one to make the government's decisions in these parts."

"I won't say I'm not flattered, but I'll have to think about it a bit."

"That's fine. I'm going out to the Fort. You discuss it with Mrs. Baines and I'll come back to talk later."

"Unfortunately, Mrs. Baines passed away a while back," he commented sadly.

"Oh, I'm sorry to hear that, Judge," replied Gus sincerely.

Gregory Baines smiled, "Judge . . . that doesn't sound too bad. You can leave your extra horses here while you go to the Fort, if you like."

"No sir, it sounds right good . . . Judge Gregory Baines. You think about that, and I'll be back directly. Thank you for your offer, but since I don't know how long I'll be gone, I'll just take my horses to the livery."

"That will be fine, Marshall."

After caring for his horses, Gus rode to the Fort where he met with General Nelson Miles. Gus asked the General about the raids of Geronimo, wondering if they were close to bringing him back to the prison. The General told him about placing Captain Henry Lawton and First Lieutenant Charles B. Gatewood in command of pursuing Geronimo and his followers and bringing them back to the reservation for the final time.

The General took a puff on his cigar, "When they were in pursuit, the troops followed Geronimo into a canyon in the Robledo Mountains over in New Mexico. Geronimo went into a cave so they decided to wait him out. Unfortunately the cave had a back entrance and he escaped again," he said shaking his head.

Gus smiled. "Kinda humiliating, I guess. Well, General, it was nice to see you again, I just wanted to get a report on Geronimo. I'll keep my eyes open as I go back to Texas. I've got a judge to appoint, so I better move along; nice visiting with you."

"Stop in anytime, Marshal Kelley. And do keep an eye open. As you know Geronimo could be anywhere."

Gus headed back to the settlement to check on, he hoped, 'Judge' Baines.

"Well, Marshal. I guess I can try this judge business. I always wished I could judge some of the cases I was prosecuting."

"I'm glad, Judge. Before I leave, I'll see to your office and any help you'll need."

"Don't you worry a bit about it, Marshall. I know just the lady to help me and I'll be perfectly fine working right here out of my house for a while. You just swear me in and give me the paperwork so everyone else will know what's going on."

Gus swore in the new judge, handed him the paperwork and said, "If you're okay with all this, then I'll head back home. I've got a long ride, and I've got a pretty little girl waiting for me when I get there. Let me know if you need something. You can get word to me in Sykesville, Texas. If you need anything right away, get it and we'll take care of the details later."

Gus watered and fed his horses at the livery and then headed home.

"Well, Pepper, another long haul and we'll be home, unless we run into Geronimo's bunch on the way," he said chuckling.

After a day's ride Gus came across a cool clear stream where willows and cottonwood trees grew in abundance. Talking to his horses, he said, "I bet you three are getting' mighty hungry, and I am too. This sure looks like the place we were meant to set up camp for a day or two."

He removed the packs and saddle and let Pepper move as he liked while he tethered the other two.

By the time Gus finished his supper and was enjoying his coffee, the sun was disappearing behind the horizon, pitching its bands of color into the still blue sky.

"This sure would be a nice time to be at home with Annie!" he mumbled. He dumped the grounds from his cup, pulled up his blanket and was soon asleep.

He slept soundly and didn't stir much all night. When he awoke, the sky was barely grey. It took a minute for his mind to register that his fire was blazing and there was the shadow of a person huddled near it. He smelled coffee.

He thought his mind was playing tricks on him, but he still slipped his revolver quietly from its holster and lay still trying to make out what the person was doing.

Satisfied that the person was just sitting there, he stood quietly and took a couple of steps toward the shadow.

"Don't make a move. I have you covered . . . who are you?"

The person by the fire didn't budge. As he slowly moved around so he could see the person, he heard a man's voice. "White eyes sit . . . have coffee."

An Indian! "You haven't told me who you are and why you're here," said Gus cautiously.

"Put gun away. I have none." He slowly pulled back both sides of his blanket to show he had no weapon.

"I come long way, and saw your small fire when wind blew coals. When fire got good, I saw your coffee pot; fix coffee."

"Okay, but who are you and where did you come from?"

With his chin held high he answered. "I Grey Buffalo. I worked for Ben Carson, Indian Agent."

"You **have** come a long way if you've come from Ben's," Gus said as he lowered his gun and grabbed a cup.

"Ben Carson say he had no need for me anymore, so I go home."

As Gus poured a cup of coffee, he asked, "You Shawnee? This used to be the Shawnee Trail before the cattle drives. Do you think the Shawnee will still be where you are going? Surely you know the Government keeps moving the tribes around."

"Not Shawnee . . . Cherokee. I go to see friend."

"A friend, eh? Do you have any supplies . . . any food . . . how have you been getting along?"

"No food; catch rabbit, soon."

"Well, you sit tight and I'll get us some breakfast, have some more coffee."

Gus proceeded to cut bacon and start it frying.

"Well, Grey Buffalo, I'm Marshall Commodore Kelley. Tell me, what did you do for the agent?"

"I was in charge of horses . . . did all . . . feed, doctor, put on shoes . . . all."

Gus looked at the man and wondered how old he might be. "Are you good at it?"

"I work my life, and for Ben Carson, eight years."

"Why did he say he didn't need you any longer?"

"Army man retires. Takes my work."

"I see. White man comes first. How set are you on seeing your friend?"

"Nothing else to do. Now have much time."

"If you have nothin' to do, would you be willin' to take care of *my* horses? I have a ranch down in Texas."

"Grey Buffalo interested . . . . how many horses?"

"I don't really know how many we have. I haven't counted them." Gus said thoughtfully. "How have you been getting' around?"

"Horse tied up stream."

"Oh, I see," said Gus as he started to gather up things, "Well, if you want the job, get your horse and let's ride. It's a long way to Texas.

Gus finished cleaning up the campsite and had just saddled Pepper when Grey Buffalo rode up.

Grey Buffalo had a pretty good looking saddle along with a bedroll and slicker, "You're outfitted okay, it seems.'

"Ben Carson gave to me when I go."

"Okay. Let's move on." Gus started out and Grey Buffalo followed, headed to Texas.

From time to time Gus checked over his shoulder. He couldn't shake the feeling of being followed.

Grey Buffalo noticed his checking the back trail, "Marshall Commodore Kelley expect company?" he asked

"Can't be too careful, ya know. Geronimo is on the loose again. And by the way, everybody calls me Gus."

"Gus watch back when should watch ahead."

"What do you mean?"

"Party of braves wait in trees."

"Doggone, Grey Buffalo, I don't see a thing. We better take cover before we ride right into them."

"Grey Buffalo will ride to them and make talk."

Gus looked at Grey Buffalo, his face was as expressionless as always, "You sure you want to do that?"

No answer came. He just nudged his horse and rode on quickly ahead. Gus watched him go and slowly eased Pepper into the trees.

He watched the old man sit his horse and talk into the trees. No one else was visible, Gus thought, *Now, was he funnin' me? Doesn't look as if there is anyone up there!*

After a few minutes, Grey buffalo turned and headed back. As he did so, at least twelve braves exited the trees, raised hands in salute and headed across country to the east. Gus watched and said out loud, "Well, I'll be doggoned. I must'a been asleep."

He started toward the old Indian, and when he was near he asked, "Did you know that bunch?"

"They Apache. Not know them, but I know parents. They need be on reservation."

"Well, believe me I'm glad you decided to come along with me."

The old man looked at Gus with an almost perceptible smile and said, "Then Gus won't mind if granddaughter comes too?"

"Gran . . . Granddaughter? What do you mean?"

"You have feeling of being followed . . . it my granddaughter."

As they both looked back, the old man raised his hand and a girl rode out from the trees a short distance behind them. She too was outfitted with nearly new equipment and tack.

Gus couldn't believe his eyes, "You mean she's been followin' us all this time?"

"I have," she said as she rode up to them.

"I did have the feelin' we were bein' followed, but couldn't ever see anyone."

She smiled and said, "Well, after all, I am Indian."

"You don't sound like an Indian, uh, ma'am."

"How is an Indian supposed to sound?"

"Okay, you got me there, but I think you know what I mean."

"I do know," she said smiling. "I went to a regular school near the reservation, because Grandfather worked for the MAN."

"I see; well, it shows."

Gus kept on looking at her, trying to figure out how old she was, because she wasn't a child. Her figure was slim, her coal black hair was in long braids to her waist, her dark eyes seemed to twinkle when she talked, and her face was like a china doll with soft ruby lips.

"Are you all right?" she asked.

Gus realized he was staring at her, "I'm sorry, ma'am. My name is Commodore Kelley, but everyone calls me Gus."

"My name means gentle breeze, but is hard to say and remember, so I am called Doe."

"Okay, Doe, I hired your grandpa to work my horses. What am I supposed to do with you?"

"We come as a package. I also can do anything he can do. After all, he taught me."

Gus lifted his hat and scratched his head. "Boy, I don't know what Annie will say about that."

"Who is Annie? Your wife?"

"No, not yet."

"But she will be soon?" she asked.

"I hope so, but I'm not sure . . . especially if I take you back with me," he muttered.

The three headed once again toward Texas. Gus was glad to have Grey Buffalo along after seeing how he handled the Indians. But he was a bit worried about taking his granddaughter home.

By evening, Gus found a place to camp that had clear, sweet water and plenty of grass for the growing number of horses.

While he was taking the horses to drink and stake them out on the good grass, Grey Buffalo and Doe had built a fire and had water going for coffee. As Gus walked up, Doe asked, "Which of these packs has the food? I didn't want to rummage through your packs 'till you said it would be okay."

Gus pointed to the pack that was his 'kitchen'. Doe took a skillet and some bacon and put them on the fire. Gus smiled as he watched her and thought, *maybe she can take Miraposa's place as Annie's house keeper. At least that's my story and I'm sticking to it!*

After the meal and cleanup, they sat around the fire as the sun dipped behind the horizon painting the puffy clouds with gold and traces of pink.

"Doe, tell me about your life on the reservation."

"Oh, we did not live on the reservation, Grandfather and I had a small house behind Mister Carson's house. I took care of Grandfather and also Mister Carson's house."

Gus took a sip of coffee and thought, *maybe, just maybe, that will be her job at Annie's. She is so beautiful . . . Awe, I don't have to worry about Annie,*

166

surely she will understand when I tell her how it all came about! He stood, "Well, I guess we had better turn in. We've got a long day tomorrow."

"Mister Kelley, I fixed your bed. It is ready for you."

"Oh, uh, gee that was mighty nice of you, Doe. I . . . uh, thanks. I'll see you in the morning," he said feeling a bit awkward.

After a few days, the awkwardness wore off and things went smoothly the rest of the trip.

Chapter Sixteen

When Gus, Grey Buffalo, and granddaughter Doe arrived in Sykesville, Gus made the decision to go directly to the 'Tree Top Ranch' and let them stay there until he came back. When no one answered the door, he asked the two of them to stay there until he got back. Then he rode on into Sykesville to the boarding house.

As Gus rode into town, he couldn't help but notice that the streets seemed to be mostly empty. Not many people doing business. He stepped off Pepper in front of the boarding house, tossed the reins over the hitching rack and stepped up on the walk. He turned toward the street to observe the lack of traffic. *The town has taken the bad news of the railroad pretty hard it seems,* he thought. Then he turned and walked inside.

"Howdy, Helen."

"Well, hello, Gus. Haven't seen you in a while, Annie's upstairs in her room. If I were you I wouldn't tarry down here. She's been pretty anxious about your being gone so long."

"Thanks, Helen." He proceeded up the stairs.

He gave a gentle knock on the door and heard, "Come on in, Helen."

He eased the door open, and when he could see that her back was turned to the door, he quietly walked into the room and slipped his arms around her waist and hugged her.

"Oh, Jim, I thought it was Helen!"

Gus spun her around to face him and exclaimed, JIM! Who is Jim?"

"You told me to get acquainted with my cowboys while you were gone."

He could see she was having a hard time keeping a straight face. "That's okay; I brought a pretty girl back with me."

"Pardon me? What do you mean? I was just kidding . . . there's no Jim."

"Well, there **is** a pretty girl," Gus said proudly.

"And just where did you find this *pretty girl?* she asked, a little disturbed.

He pulled her close. "I didn't intend to. I hired an old Indian farrier to take care of the horses, and only found out later that his granddaughter was trailin' us. I couldn't just tell her to be on her way, so I let her come along. She says he taught her to do everything he does, and besides she can cook and keep house. I thought maybe since Miraposa was goin' to have to leave, she could take her place," he suggested.

"That may work out then if you planned for her to work for *me*, not *you*. Miraposa has already left. That's why I came back to the boarding house. Is she really pretty?"

"Yes, she is, and I was really afraid to bring her home with us."

"You thought I would be upset?"

"I figured it was possible."

"She must be really pretty, then."

"Aw, I just look at her as someone that can shoe and take care of the horses."

"She must be *really, really* pretty."

"But not as pretty as you, Annie!" He pulled her close and kissed her, "You don't know how I've missed you."

"Well, I sure know how much I've missed you! It's so upsetting when you have to be gone so long. We have hardly any time together."

"I hope you will be pleased to know I mailed my resignation as I came into town this morning. You may have to support me since I will no longer be getting a check, even if they were a month late gettin' to me sometimes."

"Yes, Gus, I am pleased. Maybe I won't have to constantly worry that you will be killed or badly wounded. I don't want to be separated from you more than an hour or so."

He smiled. "You may get tired of me being around all the time, but I will have to take care of the ranches."

"You know what I mean."

"I do." He held her tightly and kissed her again, "But right now I have to go make sure the horses are taken care of."

"I thought that's why you hired the Indian!"

"It is, and his name is Grey Buffalo, but I left them at your pace instead of takin' them to my house, so I gotta go take care of all that. Since Helen is here, can you come with me?"

"I sure can . . . I've got to see the girl with whom you've spent the last three or four weeks." She had to carry him along a little longer.

"Aw, Annie, she don't mean nothin' to me. The old man had lost his job to a white man; and besides, he's been takin' care of horses all his life. I thought he would be good for the ranch."

When they were still a little way from the ranch, they could see Grey Buffalo and Doe coming out on the porch. He looked dignified with his grey hair pulled into braids hanging down from his shoulders with small bits of ribbon woven into them. His deerskin shirt was decorated with quills and beads, and his pants were tucked in his soft high top boots.

Doe stood beside him, her dress was fringed at the sleeves and the bottom, held tight at the waist with a beaded belt, and her hair was black as night in braids that hung down on each side to her waist.

"So that is your Indian lady friend?" she asked gazing at him.

"She's not my lady friend, and her name is Doe."

"No wonder you were worried . . . she really is beautiful."

"I know . . . I mean . . . aw, Annie."

"You can't have us both, Gus," she teased.

"Now you just stop it, Annie. You know I love you."

"Yes I know you do, Gus."

When they arrived at the house, Gus introduced them to Annie.

"Doe, do you think you would like to work here with me?" asked Annie.

"Oh, Miss Annie, your home is so beautiful. I would be thrilled to work with you."

"Are you sure you are Indian? You speak so well," came Annie's puzzled reply.

Doe laughed and replied, "I went to the white man's school and graduated with honors."

"That's wonderful! I think we will get along nicely. Welcome to The Tree Top Ranch. Let's go and get better acquainted."

As the girls left, Gus turned to Grey Buffalo, "Suppose you and me go look at Annie's horses. You'll be takin' care of them, too. Like I said, I don't know for sure how many we have."

As they walked toward the corral where the horses were penned, Gus paused. "Look down in the valley . . . see that place over there? That's my place, called the Commodore. We'll be takin' care of it, too."

Grey Buffalo looked and said nothing for a few moments, and then, "You have much to take care of," he said, feeling a bit overwhelmed.

"Don't worry you won't have to take care of it by yourself. You will have help. Mostly, I'd like for you to see that it's done right. Supervise I guess you might say."

"Grey Buffalo understand," he responded, nodding his head.

Soon both ranches were operating smoothly. Gus decided to take Pepper for a morning ride to the Tree Top. When he arrived, Doe was standing on the porch.

"Hello, Mister, Kelley."

Gus stepped down and walked to the porch. "Are things goin' okay, Doe?"

"Things are going very well, Mister Kelley."

"Just call me Gus, Doe."

"When Miss Annie talks about you she calls you Mister Kelley."

"I see, well, you can call me Gus if you want to."

"Thank you. Oh, Mrs. Kelley has gone to town."

"She has? I guess I'll head that way, then," he said as he turned toward his horse, then he stopped short and said, "By the way, she's not Mrs. Kelley yet."

"I know but she soon will be."

Gus just smiled, nodded his head, mounted up and rode to town.

When Gus arrived at the boarding house, he went directly to Annie's room and knocked.

"Come in."

When he entered she turned toward him with a big smile. "Guess what?"

"I can't imagine, but with that smile I'll bet it's good."

"I sold the boarding house!"

"You did? Well, that's great, Annie!"

"Isn't it? Helen and I have taken care of everything."

'We should celebrate. I'll get Emilio to barbecue some steaks and we'll invite all our friends. How does that sound?"

"That sounds fine, Gus."

"Do you have a ride home?" he asked.

"Yes, Grey Buffalo saddled the little roan for me."

"Well then, I'll go invite folks and go to get things started."

"Gus."

"Yes?"

"Be sure to ask Charlie Wong."

"Will do." He kissed her and started to leave when he turned back and held her while he kissed her hard again, "I don't want to leave."

"Gus, you have to, because there is nothing you can do here right now!" she said smiling.

"Oh, all right." He turned and left, reluctantly.

Chapter Seventeen

Later that day after Annie got home' she was in her bedroom changing clothes. Doe was out at the barn gathering eggs. When Annie heard the front door latch click and the big oak door open and then close, she shouted from her bedroom, "Doe? . . . Gus is that you?"

No answer came. "I'll be out in a minute," she added.

As she continued changing, her bedroom door creaked slightly. When she turned, a strange man was standing in the doorway grinning.

"Who are you? What are you doing here? What do you want?"

He didn't answer, but moved toward her, a sadistic grin plastered on his face. She backed away until she ran into the bed and sat down. She started to rise.

He moved quickly and shoved her back on the bed. Then he placed his knees against her legs to keep her from getting up. He unbuckled his gun belt and let it drop to the floor and his knees moved. Then he unbuckled his belt and dropped his pants to the top of his boots. That is when Annie raised both legs, put her foot in his stomach and pushed as hard as she could. With his pants down around his boot tops, he was hobbled and fell back on the floor.

Annie quickly did a back flip over the bed to the other side and came around the bed trying to get to the door. As she passed him, he reached out and caught her ankle. She fell to the floor, and he began to pull her toward him with one hand while trying to unwrap his pants from the top of his boots so he could move.

While he kept trying to pull her toward him she stretched out her arm toward his gun belt. He continued fumbling with his pants and yanking on her arm, so she stretched further, until she could feel the leather.

Annie continued to stretch and kick until she could feel the cold steel of his gun. She quickly pulled it into her hand and cocked it.

When he heard the clicks of the Colt, he looked at her face with a questioning look. Annie closed her eyes and pulled the trigger.

Blood splattered across the room and on Annie's clothes. The man collapsed on her. She pushed him off and ran out the door.

Doe, having heard the shot, came running into the house. She saw Annie trembling and covered in blood. Doe screamed and ran to her.

Annie quickly said, "I'm all right, Doe. I'm going to the Commodore. Don't go into the bedroom."

When Annie ran out the door and saw the man's horse tied out front, she jumped into the saddle and rode as fast as she could to the Commodore Ranch house.

When she rushed inside, Gus was in the living room and saw all the blood on her clothes. She ran into his arms.

"Are you hurt," he asked, "What happened?"

She was crying so hard she could hardly speak. "Oh, Gus, I never want to go into the Tree Top again!"

"Why, Annie? . . . What has happened, are you sure you are not hurt?"

"Oh Gus, it was horrible. He just walked in . . . I thought it was Doe or you."

"Who walked in, Annie?"

"I don't know who he was."

She quickly explained what happened, and Gus called for Rosita to help get the blood washed off.

"I'll go take care of it, and send Doe back with some of your clothes. Sheriff Lacy is coming out anyway . . . we'll take care of it. Are you *sure* you are not hurt?"

"No, I'm not hurt, Gus . . . go . . . I'll be all right, Rosita is here.

"I'll be back as soon as I can."

When Gus had taken care of things at the Tree Top Ranch, he returned home. Annie was sitting in one of the wide, heavy leather chairs by the fireplace.

"Annie, how are you doing?" He slipped into the big chair beside her.

"A lot better now, but who was that man? Why was he in my house?

It was one of Hawk's men. I recognized him. He apparently avoided capture when the other men were arrested. I don't think there are any more left to bother either of us, Annie. At least I sure hope not. Do you still want to celebrate?"

I don't want this to spoil things. Yes, I still want to celebrate, but, Gus, I don't think I can stay over there after this. I shudder to think I might have lost what I was saving all my life for you."

"Annie, honey, you won't have to. This is your home now. We can use that place for other things. Just don't worry about it. I want you here anyway; we'll be married soon."

He placed his arm around her, and she placed her head on his shoulder, "Will we ever be rid of Hawk and Roscoe?" she asked, "It seems that somehow they are trying to take it all back and get rid of us."

"It just feels that way, Annie, Those two are gone, and you probably took care of the last one of the bunch."

He turned her, pulled her across his lap and cradled her head in the bend of his arm. He then gently lifted her face and touched her lips with his fingers. She sighed and arched up to meet his lips with a kiss. He gently bit her lips with his and felt her body shake, he kissed her harder and then pulled away.

"This can only lead to trouble," he said, regretfully "All those folks I invited will be here soon . . . we need to get busy. Did Doe bring everything you need? You're sure you are okay."

"Yes, I'm fine and she did, Gus. I told her to work here with Rosita. Neither of us wants to go back there . . . at least for a while."

"I'm sure Rosita will appreciate the help."

The sky was aglow from the setting sun, and flames licked into the sky over the steaks that Emilio had on the large outdoor grill.

Rosita and Doe were laboring over the beans and potato salad and other fixings for the celebration.

Sheriff Lacy was chatting with Charlie Wong, and Gus was laughing with Harve Tobek about his not being able to figure out who Gus was.

Rice Stanford and LaRice pulled up in their buckboard, and Gus walked out to meet them. "I'm glad you two could make it. Get down and someone will take care of your horses. Dinner should be ready before long. "LaRice, I'm sorry no one your age has arrived yet, but make yourself at home. They should be coming along soon, and Rice, thank you for comin'."

Rice was watching the flames jumping above the big grill, "Why, I wouldn't have missed it for anything."

Gus was walking among the guests when he noticed a small group listening to Grey Buffalo and looking toward the north sky. He walked close so he could hear what was being said.

"It called Big Dipper, but do you know how it got there?" asked Grey Buffalo.

"No," several voices in the group responded.

"The story of the Cheyenne, passed down through the ages, tell of a princess of my people that was able to make beautiful clothes from smooth white deer skins and quills and with many adornments. She knew not why, but she made six complete outfits for braves and one that was smaller, and then she made one for herself. She packed them on her father's horse, and when her mother asked where she was going she said, 'I'm taking them to my brothers.'

"'But dear, you have no brothers.'

"'I will when I get to where they are!'

"When she arrived at another camp, a small boy ran out to meet her. "'I am here to be your sister, and I have brought fine clothes for you.' As she opened the package of fine clothes, the young man's six brothers came out and the clothes fit perfectly.

"Others of the tribe were very jealous of the fine clothes and came to them and said, 'Give us the girl so she can make fine clothes for us.'

"But the small boy had powers and told them that she would not come out.

"His brothers told the small boy to use his powers to make them go away.

"As many more from the tribe came and got very loud, his brothers asked him again to use his powers.

"'I am,' the boy said. 'Go climb the sycamore tree,' and they did, but the people pushed hard on the tree until it was being pushed over.

"The boy said, 'hold hands." When they held hands they were turned into stars, and gave off very bright light and began to rise up into the sky. Together they formed that which you call the Big Dipper. The girl is the brightest star and the young boy is the little one at the end of the dipper."

A couple of "awws" were heard, and Gus saw that the whole crowd was looking toward the North sky.

After the meal, Gus moved to where Annie was visiting with a few of the ladies. He took her hand and then he stepped up on the dance floor that had been erected. "Can I have everyone's attention?"

Everyone quieted down and moved toward the platform.

"I would like to thank everyone for comin', and I would like you to know that I have asked the beautiful Annabelle Shaw to be my wife . . . and she has accepted." Cheers and applause followed.

He stepped down by Annie and put his arm around her as they were being congratulated.

When the hand shaking slowed down Gus whispered to Annie, "How are you doing?"

"I'm doing okay, but I think I'll try to go to bed early . . . I am feeling a bit exhausted."

"I'll tell Doe to get a room ready for you."

"No, Gus, It wouldn't look right . . . we aren't married yet, and I wouldn't want anyone to think that . . . well, you know."

Gus smiled and said, "Yes, I know."

"I'll go in and stay at the boarding house until the wedding," she said.

"I'll tell Emilio to have one of the men get the buggy ready, and I'll come in to have breakfast with you tomorrow."

He kissed her, which brought a few 'awws' from the ladies at the party.

Gus saw to it that Annie was taken care of, then he scanned the crowd for Estefan Romero who had come out from San Angelo.

Gus spotted him and made his way across the crowd. "Ah, Estefan," Gus said as he approached. "I haven't been ignoring you. I just wanted to wait until you were filled with barbecue."

"Si, Señor Kelley. I have managed well," He said patting his stomach.

"I am glad you got my message and were able to come to visit."

"Yes, and your nice celebration has been a very interesting surprise."

"My friend and now judge . . . David Berkshire told me that you were retiring from your work in San Angelo and are looking for a place to retire."

"This is true; a place in the country, like this you have here."

"That's why I wrote to you. Miss Shaw owns the ranch next to here and I would like for you to be my guest for a few days . . . I have something to show you that I think you will like."

"I would like that very much, Señor Kelley."

"Well, I have to run into town first thing in the morning and that will give you time for a leisurely breakfast and a second cup of coffee; then we will get together."

"Bueno, Señor Kelley."

"Then, in the mornin' it is."

Gus rode in early to have breakfast with Annie at the boarding house. He gave a gentle knock on her door, "Annie . . . are you awake? It's Gus," he said in a low voice.

"Yes, Gus, I'll be right out."

At breakfast they sat in the far corner. "Annie, I didn't tell you and I hope you don't mind."

"What is it, Gus?" she asked curiously.

"I asked Estefan Romero, of San Angelo, to come to our party last night."

"I think I met him: tall, distinguished looking, with a little grey in the temples?" she interrupted.

"Yes, that's him. Anyway David Berkshire said he was looking for a place to retire and move to the country. He was tired of city life. I think he was over-seeing land for the Mexican Government, or something. I asked him to come because I wanted to show him the Tree Top house . . . not all the land and stuff, just the house and a few out-buildings. What do you think?"

"Oh, Gus, that would be great. I could visit the place. I just can't stay there," she said with a shudder. "Do you think he will be interested?"

"Yes, I think so. I'll need the papers in order to draw up a new agreement that will show exactly what the sale would include."

"They are in the safe, I'll get them. Oh, Gus, this is great. I hope it all works out."

Gus returned to the Commodore Ranch and found Estefan relaxing on the back porch watching some of the men breaking horses. "I guess you got a good breakfast this morning."

"Yes I did! I may want to steal Rosita and Doe; they treated me as if I were important."

"They take care of all of us that way. We are lucky to have them. Do you feel like taking a short ride this morning?"

"Why, yes I do. I was hoping that you would ask. I must say I have enjoyed this get-away very much."

Gus smiled, "Then I hope you will enjoy what I plan to show you. Let's go out front; our horses should be ready."

Gus had already asked Emilio to saddle Pepper and the buckskin and bring them around front.

They were waiting when Gus and Estefan walked through the front door.

"You said you are looking for a place to retire. A place like this, in the country."

"That is true. Your ranch is exactly what I had in mind, but not with all the land and things to take care of. I am getting too old for all that."

"Well, I may just have what you want."

Gus picked up the pace and Estefan followed. As they rode up the hill, The Tree Top came into view. They rode into the courtyard and up to the house. "Let's get down," said Gus, as he stepped off Pepper.

Gus took a key from above the huge oak door and unlocked it. Then he led Estefan into the large living room.

"What do you think of this place, Estefan? All the furnishings go with it." Gus led him through the house so that he could see it was almost identical to the Commodore house.

"This is what you wanted to show me? It is so much like the other!" exclaimed Estefan.

"Yes, it is. It belongs to Annie and we would be pleased to have you as a neighbor. It will be only the house and a few out-buildings for your riding stock and other necessary things like chickens and a cow or two. The rest we will keep."

"Señor Kelley, I don't know how you knew, but this is exactly what I had hoped to find." Estefan said in amazement.

"If that's the case, we can draw up the papers, and the place is yours. We've named it the Tree Top Ranch because it was higher than the Commodore

Ranch, kinda above the trees there, but you call it what you want."

That evening, at the boarding house, Gus met with Annie for dinner. "Annie, Estefan wants the Tree Top and I will go into San Angelo to meet with him next week. Then we need to plan the wedding."

"Oh, Gus, that sounds so good, it seems we have waited so long".

Chapter Eighteen

"Annie, while Paul is getting' the buckboard ready for ya'll to travel in, I'm goin' to ride on to San Angelo and get enough rooms reserved in the hotel for everybody that's goin' to be in the wedding. Just to make sure I got it, there's Helen and her brother Burt, Harve and you and me. Everybody else said they would take care of their own"

"That sounds right," she said smiling.

"One more thing before you go, Gus. Will you go by Mister Wong's and pick up my dress? It will be ready, I can't wait for you to see it . . . but don't look at it now!"

"I promise I won't look; I'll bring it by here, and then I'll see you in San Angelo."

"And, Gus, don't reserve your room as long as you do the others," she said coyly.

It took a moment for it to register what she meant. He dazzled her with a broad smile, gave her a kiss and headed out the door.

When he arrived in San Angelo, he reserved the rooms at the hotel and rode to Judge David Berkshire's house. David was going to perform the ceremony. Then he reserved the chapel.

The day of the wedding, Gus, and his best man, Bob Lacy, along with Helen, Annie's maid of honor; stood in front of Judge Berkshire among the flowers waiting for the bride to enter. When she did, Gus couldn't believe his eyes. *That I could be marryin' a lady this beautiful is somethin' I'm not sure that I can comprehend.*

The service was beautiful. The sun dipped below the horizon just as he kissed his bride. The sun's rays shot through the low hanging clouds and gave a golden glow to the faces of all who were present.

After the ceremony and reception, Annie went to her room, and sat where she could look out the window at the moon and the stars. Soon she removed the dress and carefully put it in its box, then slipped on her night gown. As she was putting the box away, Gus knocked gently and entered. Light from the candle in his hand fell across her face and his heart began to beat faster.

Gus blew out the candle and closed the door. Moonlight flooded the room and surrounded her in a pale glow. Gus was spellbound.

"Well, Gus, are you just going to stand there?"

"Of all the beauty in nature that I have seen, none can compare with the beauty I see in you."

His words sent a thrill through her entire body.

He approached her, took her warm body in his arms and kissed her. As he held her, he felt her trembling, so he pulled her closer, and gently pressed his lips to hers. She could feel his readiness and arched against him even tighter. His heart was racing as he placed his arms behind her back and under her knees. He, lifted her up, and with a gentle kiss, placed her on the bed and slipped in beside her.

* * * *

Settling The West